GOLDEN SUNDOWN

When Marshal Lincoln Hawk headed towards Sweetwater with rancher Truman Garner, they were being trailed by the Calhoun gang. They believed that Garner knew the location of stolen gold. When the gang captures Truman and delivers an ultimatum — hand over the gold by sundown or die — Lincoln has to ensure that the threat is not delivered. And then there are raiders who plan to wrest the gold from the Calhoun gang. Lincoln knows there'll be one hell of a showdown come that golden sundown.

SCOTT CONNOR

GOLDEN SUNDOWN

Complete and Unabridged

LINFORD
Leicester

First published in Great Britain in 2005 by
Robert Hale Limited
London

First Linford Edition
published 2006
by arrangement with
Robert Hale Limited
London

British Library CIP Data

Connor, Scott
   Golden sundown.—Large print ed.—
Linford western library
1. Western stories
2. Large type books
I. Title
823.9'2 [F]

ISBN 1–84617–317–5

Published by
F. A. Thorpe (Publishing)
Anstey, Leicestershire

Set by Words & Graphics Ltd.
Anstey, Leicestershire
Printed and bound in Great Britain by
T. J. International Ltd., Padstow, Cornwall

This book is printed on acid-free paper

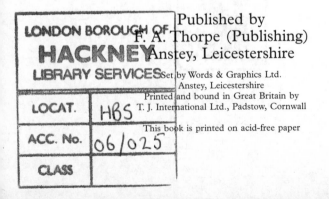

1

'Is that it?' Crane Powell asked.

'They say Truman Garner now owns the ridge outside Sweetwater,' Elwood said. He peered up at the ridge, then shrugged. 'And that might be it.'

Crane hurled his spade to the ground. 'Decide, damn you.'

'Yeah,' Rocco muttered, cracking his knuckles. He brushed past Crane and the last member of their group, Wallace, and slammed a hand on Elwood's shoulder. 'And if you get it wrong, I'll bury you so deep, your body will never see daylight again.'

Elwood glanced at Rocco's hand, then shrugged from under it and ran his gaze along the ridge, then back to the smaller promontory to his side.

'Decker said he headed to Sweetwater, then rode west for twelve miles until he reached a ridge. On the other side was a forest, and — '

'And we know the story,' Rocco roared. He grabbed Elwood's collar and pulled him up to his chest so that he could stare straight into his eyes. 'We've had twenty long years dreaming about it and we don't need to hear it again. So for the last time — is that the ridge Decker told you about?'

Elwood squirmed in Rocco's grip, but finding no give, he slumped.

'Yeah,' he said, his voice shaking. Then he coughed and firmed his voice. 'Yeah, that's the ridge all right. No doubt about it.'

'Good,' Rocco muttered and threw Elwood back a pace.

'Probably.'

Rocco whirled round, his eyes blazing.

'You what?'

Elwood raised his hands, smiling. 'Only joking. That's the ridge all right.'

Rocco pointed at his thin-lipped scowl. 'Do I look amused?'

'Quit arguing, you two,' Crane said.

He raised his hands and took a long pace to stand between Rocco and Elwood. When he received a reluctant nod from Rocco, he swung his spade on to his shoulder. 'Come on. We got ourselves some digging to do.'

Crane turned and scampered up the slope leading to the ridge, closely followed by Elwood, who, with a last glance at the scowling Rocco, hurried on to draw alongside.

Rocco exchanged a pained glare with Wallace then both men turned and headed up the slope after them, their spades slung over their shoulders.

The ridge was angular, monolithic outcroppings of rock thrusting up into the clear blue sky, but the stark beauty was lost on Crane and his men. As they trudged over the slippery scree at the slope bottom, the four men adopted the same downbeat postures that their twenty-year stint in Barton jail had thrust upon them.

But as they neared the top of the ridge, their stooped backs straightened and they hurried. And by the time they were within a stone's throw of the top, they were running, a combination of excitement and anticipation making them stamp their feet to the ground and create a huge trailing plume of dust.

Crane and Elwood whooped their delight, Wallace joined in after a moment, and then finally even Rocco uttered a long whoop and barged past Crane to crest the ridge in the lead.

All four men shared a breathless race across the craggy ridge top, rounding boulders and vaulting smaller rocks in their haste to be the first to reach the other side. They hurled up yet more dust as they kicked and hollered their way across the top, even their craggy faces smoothing as they seemed to become younger in a matter of moments.

Rocco gained a ten-yard advantage, but at the end of the ridge he slid to a halt when a near 200 foot sheer drop confronted him. His arms wheeled as he fought for balance. Then he edged back three paces to a safer position and waved at the other men to join him.

As the others flanked him, he peered down at the land below, his face wreathed in a huge smile.

The smile froze, then died.

The spade fell from his slack fingers.

He staggered back two paces, barging into Wallace and Elwood. His mouth opened and closed but no words emerged.

With a sickness descending into his guts, Crane paced past him to peer down the side of the ridge.

The plains stretched ahead until they merged into mist-shrouded mountains on the horizon, but wherever he looked there were no trees.

Elwood and Wallace pushed Rocco aside and followed the direction of Crane's gaze. As one, they winced.

'You got it wrong, Elwood,' Rocco roared. 'There ain't no forest.'

'I didn't,' Elwood murmured, tipping back his hat. 'I surely didn't.'

'Then where's the trees?' Rocco glanced at his fist, then shrugged and advanced on Elwood with it raised.

In a reflex action, Elwood raised his forearm, but Rocco batted it aside and slammed a round-armed slug to Elwood's cheek that sent him sprawling.

For once, Crane didn't stop the impetuous Rocco from acting on his festering anger. Instead, he folded his arms as Rocco dragged Elwood to his feet then held him upright and slugged his jaw, knocking him on his back.

Only when Rocco ripped back his foot ready to kick his frustration out of Elwood did Crane raise a hand.

'Enough,' he said. 'This ain't helping us.'

'Helping us!' Rocco snorted. 'Who says it's helping us? I'm just enjoying myself.'

Rocco thundered his boot into Elwood's guts, Elwood folding over the blow, then grabbed his collar and tugged him to his knees. He gathered a firmer grip of his collar, then dragged him on hands and feet to the ridge edge. There, he pulled him upright and pushed him forward so he dangled over the side of the ridge.

'It's there. It has to be,' Elwood babbled, his feet scrambling for purchase on the rock-strewn surface.

The displaced rocks cascaded from under his feet and with slow, inevitable momentum, clattered down the sheer side of the ridge and disappeared below, their clattering echoes not sounding for another few seconds.

'Put him down,' Crane snapped, pacing to Rocco's side.

'If you insist.' Rocco chuckled and thrust Elwood out a foot further. 'I reckon he can look for the forest on his way down.'

'You ain't doing that. Elwood is the only one who knows the directions.'

'And I followed them,' Elwood screeched.

Rocco pointed down. 'Then why is there no forest down there?'

Elwood's gaze followed the direction of Rocco's pointing. He shook his head, but then his eyes narrowed and he leaned down.

'Let me go,' he whispered. 'I didn't get it wrong.'

Rocco glanced at him, then pulled him back from the edge and peered in the same direction.

'What you looking at?'

Elwood hunkered down, then hefted a stone and hurled it, aiming for a grouping of boulders some hundred yards away. The stone fell far short, but he watched it and the stones it displaced, until the terrain's former stillness prevailed over the sudden ripple of activity.

Then he pointed at a small building, the only visible man-made object.

'Because this *is* the right place. And I guess Truman Garner has made some changes in the last twenty years.'

Crane knelt beside him. 'Then we can go down and get it?'

'Nope,' Elwood murmured with a pronounced gulp. 'Trouble is, I reckon it's long gone.'

★ ★ ★

Seymour Fry's right eye was twitching.

Marshal Lincoln Hawk still ordered a whiskey from him, then leaned back on the counter and glanced around the trading post.

The post was only fifteen miles out of Sweetwater, but with dense fog enveloping the plains and with progress becoming increasingly slow over the last two hours, the stagecoach driver had insisted that they stop here.

Aside from Lincoln's fellow traveller — a rancher, who was wandering around the post's wares — the only other customers were four grey-haired men who were sharing a low conversation by the back wall. These men had dirt-encrusted spades slung over their shoulders and from their ragged clothing and sour expressions, Lincoln judged them to be unsuccessful prospectors.

Seymour slammed a glass on the counter, and with slow movements,

Lincoln threw a coin to him and took the whiskey. As Lincoln tipped back his hat, he exchanged a glance with him.

With a nonchalant swipe of his towel along the counter, Seymour flicked his gaze over Lincoln's shoulder at the prospectors by the back wall, then back to Lincoln.

Lincoln nodded, then turned and leaned back on the counter. He took a long sip of his drink and bared his teeth, relishing his first whiskey in two days of slow travelling.

From the corner of his eye, he noted that the tallest of the prospectors was staring at him, but when he let his gaze wander past him, the man looked away.

He expected this man to confront him immediately, but it was a full minute before, with a last low muttered order to his fellow prospectors, the man sauntered across the clear area to Lincoln's side. He leaned on the counter, matching Lincoln's casual stance.

Lincoln tipped his hat as he turned to him.

'Howdy,' he said.

'Howdy. Name's Crane Powell.' He shuffled a pace closer to Lincoln and rubbed his chin as he glanced around the trading post. 'You just passing through?'

'Yep. Stagecoach is heading for Sweetwater.'

Crane smiled with just his mouth. 'I'm waiting for a man who's heading to Sweetwater.'

Lincoln shrugged. 'Plenty of people head to Sweetwater.'

Crane glanced at the door, then swung round to stand before Lincoln so that if Lincoln were to walk in any direction he'd have to barge past him.

'They do, but you have the look of the man I'm waiting for.' Crane licked his lips and stood tall. 'I reckon you're Truman Garner.'

'Sorry, friend.' Lincoln took a sip of his drink as, from the corner of his eye, he watched the rancher back so that he leaned against a heap of provisions bags. 'You got the wrong man.'

Crane grunted his disbelief, then glanced over his shoulder and nodded.

As he turned back, the other three prospectors sauntered across the room to flank him.

'And I reckon I'm right.' Crane rolled his shoulders.

Lincoln glanced along the arc of men.

Despite their age, the men all stared at him with eager grins and bright eyes shining from their grimed faces. And although Lincoln judged that the youngest of them was more than ten years older than himself, they had the lean build of men who had worked hard and survived tough times.

Lincoln shrugged and transferred the glass to his left hand. He smiled, but the man to his right, Rocco, cracked his knuckles.

Lincoln still raised the glass to his mouth, then stopped with it brushing his lips and hurled the whiskey in Crane's face.

As Crane spluttered and staggered

forward, Lincoln dropped the glass and swung his fist back-handed into Crane's guts knocking him to the side, then charged the nearest two men, Elwood and Wallace. With his arms raised high, he grabbed each man in a neck hold, bent them double, and hammered their heads together.

Even before they'd hit the floor, Lincoln had swung round, but it was to face a pulled gun from Rocco. Lincoln glared hard at him, then lifted his hands to chest level with the palms facing down.

'Ain't no need for that,' he murmured. 'We just have ourselves a minor misunderstanding.'

Crane rolled to his feet, wiping the whiskey from his face and freeing a clear area of wrinkled skin, then pulled his gun too and aimed it at Lincoln's chest. With a short twirl of his hand, Crane gestured for Lincoln to remove his gunbelt.

Lincoln glared at Crane a moment, then with deliberately slow movements, unhooked his belt and let it fall at his feet. He kicked it along the floor, but with just enough force to ensure it stopped midway between Crane and himself.

Lincoln transferred his weight to his left leg, ready to kick Crane when he bent for the belt, but Crane gestured for Lincoln to back two paces, then ordered Elwood to pick it up.

'Ain't no minor misunderstanding here, Truman,' Crane said. 'And unless you tell me the truth, you'll get a bullet in the guts.'

Lincoln glanced to the corner of the trading post where the rancher had now huddled with the stagecoach driver. He directed a short shake of his head towards them, then let his shoulders slump.

'All right. You've found me. I'm Truman Garner. Just tell what you want and we can sort this out.'

'Wait!' the rancher shouted.

Crane glanced to the side. 'For what?'

14

Lincoln flashed the rancher a harsh glare, but the rancher shook his head, then shrugged his jacket straight and stood tall.

'Because,' he said, taking a long pace forwards, 'you have the wrong man. That man is Lincoln Hawk.'

Crane nodded. 'And who are you?'

The rancher strode across the trading post to stand before Crane. He smiled.

'I'm Truman Garner.'

2

Crane spat on the floor, then swirled round to glare at Lincoln.

'Now,' he muttered, 'why did you go and say that you were Truman if you ain't?'

Lincoln shrugged. 'Kind of reckoned you wouldn't listen to what I said no matter what I claimed.'

Crane chuckled. 'You probably reckoned right. But I still — '

'Your quarrel with Lincoln is irrelevant,' Truman said, striding two long paces to stand between Crane and Lincoln. He held his back straight and his chin aloft. 'If you have a problem with me, just state your business.'

Crane glared over Truman's shoulder at Lincoln a moment longer, then turned his gaze on Truman.

'I reckon you know what that is.' Crane raised his eyebrows. 'From what

I've heard, you're the richest man in Sweetwater.'

Truman raised on his heels. His shining boots creaked as he nodded.

'I am at that. I am at that.' Truman stood firm, but a long sigh escaped his lips as he appraised Crane and the other men. 'And I suppose I understand your business. But I'll be a disappointment to you: I have nothing of value on me.'

'I don't believe that.' Crane roved his gaze to the silver-plated watch dangling from Truman's waistcoat pocket.

Truman lowered his gaze to consider the watch, then with a shrug, unhooked it from his waistcoat.

'I do have this.' Truman leaned back to place it on the counter beside Rocco. 'And if you gentlemen will just leave, you can have it.'

'Obliged.' Crane glanced at the watch. 'But that still ain't enough.'

Truman patted his jacket from top to bottom, then raised his hands. 'I have nothing else.'

To a flicked gesture from Crane, Rocco strode to Truman's side and looked him up and down, then ripped open his jacket. He rummaged in the pockets, then patted the lining.

Throughout Rocco's searching, Truman kept his jaw firm, flaring his eyes only when Rocco's over-eager poking ripped through the lining.

But within a minute, Rocco stood back, muttering his failure to find anything of value. Then he snorted and roved his gaze to the side until it rested on Lincoln.

'I reckon he just needs some persuading,' he gibbered. He holstered his gun, then swaggered along the counter.

Lincoln stood his ground with his jaw clenched tight, but Rocco still lunged for his arm. Lincoln struggled but Rocco wrapped a dirty hand around his forearm and dragged him a pace along the counter.

'I got nothing of value either,' Lincoln grunted, digging his heels in and resisting Rocco's tugging.

Rocco chuckled. 'I don't care what you got. You can show Truman what he'll get if he don't start being right co-operative.'

'Take your hands off him,' Truman said, swirling round to confront Rocco with his fists opening and closing. 'Your quarrel is with me.'

Rocco sneered and dragged Lincoln another pace, but with a sudden lunge, Lincoln ripped his arm free.

In a short action, Lincoln hurled a fist at Rocco's face, but Rocco threw up a hand, catching the fist by his cheek. But even as he yanked the hand down towards his side, Lincoln hurled up his left hand and this time he was fast enough to catch Rocco a stinging chop to the cheek that rocked his head to the side.

Rocco grunted and wrenched Lincoln's right arm down, aiming to twist it behind his back, but Lincoln flexed his shoulders and halted Rocco's progress. Even as Lincoln strained and began to twist Rocco's arm instead, Crane strode across the trading post to stand beside Rocco.

'Truman's right,' he said. 'Our quarrel is with him. Release this man.'

'But he — '

'Release him! Or you'll get more than just a slap.'

With a muttered oath, Rocco threw Lincoln away from him.

Lincoln staggered back to slam into the counter, then straightened his jacket and fixed Rocco with his firm gaze.

'Any other orders?' Rocco muttered.

Crane glanced at Lincoln, who returned a defiant sneer, then swung up his left fist, the blow crunching into the point of Rocco's chin.

The blow was only strong enough to knock his teeth together, but still Rocco firmed his jaw, his fists clenched tight as he advanced a pace to confront Crane.

'Yeah,' Crane muttered, 'you don't threaten anyone but Truman, and you don't even think of arguing with me.'

Rocco rocked forward, but as Crane

met his gaze with his own level stare, Rocco glanced away, then stalked past him to stand by the counter, muttering under his breath.

Crane stood a moment, then turned to Truman and raised his eyebrows.

'Obliged for your decency,' Truman said. 'But I'll still be a disappointment to you.'

Crane sauntered a pace closer to Truman.

'You won't. I reckon you have a lot more than that watch.'

Truman flashed a wan smile. 'As you have acted with decency, you can have this too.'

Truman slipped a hand into his jacket and rooted around deep within the confines of the lining to emerge with a leather wallet. As Rocco grunted his irritation, he extracted a billfold and dropped it on the counter beside the watch.

Crane edged to the counter and poked the billfold open, then snorted.

'This still ain't enough.'

'It's all I have — around fifty dollars.'

'If you want us to leave, you'll give me something more substantial than that.' Crane grinned and set his feet far apart. 'You own thousands of acres of land, thousands of head of cattle, and most of Sweetwater.'

'I do, and if you want me to sell you some land so you can earn an honest living, I'll break a habit of a lifetime and offer you good terms, but I own nothing you'd think of as valuable.' Truman pointed over Crane's shoulder at the door and raised his voice so that it echoed through the trading post. 'So, just take the money and the watch. And because you acted with some decency, you'll hear no more about it.'

'I ain't going nowhere until you give me what I want.' Crane raised his gun to aim it at Truman's chest.

Seymour uttered a strangulated squeal and Lincoln edged a pace closer to Crane, but Truman flashed only the shortest of glances at the gun. If it concerned him, he gave no sign as he met Crane's gaze.

'Then just tell me what that is.'

'You know what I want. You always knew someone would come and reclaim their property. You just didn't know when it'd happen, or who it'd be.' Crane smiled. 'And now, it's happened. And it's me.'

Truman narrowed his eyes. 'I don't know what you mean. All I can give you is fifty dollars and that watch.'

'Then we got ourselves a problem, because I want one hell of a lot more than that.'

'How much?'

Crane rolled his gaze around the trading post, glancing at Seymour, the driver, Lincoln, then settling on Truman.

'Fifty thousand dollars,' he whispered.

Truman snorted a laugh. 'You trying to be funny?'

'I ain't. That's what I've come for, and that's what you'll give me.' Crane looked at Rocco with an exaggerated turn of his head, forcing Truman to follow his gaze. 'Or I'll let Rocco ask you for the money, and as you've seen, he ain't nowhere near as polite as I am.'

'If I were to sell everything I own,' Truman said, his voice raised and high-pitched for the first time, 'it'd take years to find a buyer. And even then, I'd get nowhere near fifty thousand dollars.'

'You're worth at least that.' With the barrel of his gun, Crane tipped back his hat. 'And I know how you came by that much wealth.'

'And so does everyone in Sweetwater: it was by hard work.' Truman glanced at Rocco and sneered. 'And that's something you and your worthless friends wouldn't know about.'

'For the last twenty years we've worked harder than you ever will, and we did all that work for you.'

Truman narrowed his eyes. 'I don't understand.'

'Then I'll remind you — twenty years ago, Decker Calhoun raided a gold shipment bound for Texas.' Crane stalked in a short circle, patting his free hand against his leg. 'He stole fifty thousand dollars' worth of gold bars. But the authorities put Marshal Zandana on his trail, and with the marshal closing and the gold slowing him down, he buried the gold, aiming to come back for it later. But he never got the chance. The marshal caught him and he got life in Barton jail. But Decker didn't talk and nobody found the gold.'

'I've heard that story,' Truman said, his voice low and guarded.

'Zandana then tracked down the rest of the Calhoun gang. Those that lived got twenty years.'

Truman nodded as he appraised Crane. 'And I guess you four men are what's left of the Calhoun gang. And you've served your sentence.'

'You guessed right.' Crane strode a pace closer to Truman and smiled. 'You want to finish the story for me?'

'I can't. I don't know what you want with me.' Truman held his hands wide. 'You'll have to spell it out.'

'Calhoun buried the gold twelve miles out of Sweetwater in a forest beside a ridge. Except when we arrived to dig it up three days ago, we found that the ridge is now on your land and worse, you'd cleared the trees.'

'I cleared plenty of land.'

'I know, but either way, the gold ain't there no more. Except the rancher who now owns the land just happens to be one of the richest men in the state. And I just don't believe in coincidence.'

'I got wealthy from my own efforts, not from a stash of stolen gold.'

Crane glanced at Rocco and gave him the barest of nods.

Moving with a speed that would be impressive for a man half his age, Rocco stormed two long paces and lunged. With a large fist, he grabbed Truman's collar and pulled him up straight, forcing him to stand on tiptoes.

'Everyone's just heard what Crane's accused you of doing,' he grunted, hurling back a fist. 'And we can't walk away from this now. So, if you keep on pushing us, I'll do something you won't enjoy, but I will. Now talk!'

Truman struggled, but finding that Rocco's grip was firm, he looked away.

Then, inch by inch, his shoulders slumped and it may have been a trick of the light, but Lincoln was sure that the hair poking out from beneath his hat greyed as he watched. And when Truman spoke, his voice was tired and gruff, none of his former confidence remaining.

'I suppose I'm relieved this is finally over,' he murmured. 'But I won't talk to you until — '

'You will,' Rocco roared, spit flying from his mouth to splatter over Truman's face.

Truman gulped back his distaste, but then met Rocco's gaze.

'You didn't let me finish. I *will* talk to you, but only after I've returned to Sweetwater and talked to my wife.'

'What?'

'I don't care what the likes of you want, but I do care for my wife's opinion of me and I need to tell her about this before someone else does.'

Rocco glared down at Truman a moment longer, then glanced at Crane and when Crane nodded, he released Truman with a snap of his wrist and using mock care, smoothed Truman's rumpled jacket.

'You're in no position to order anyone to do anything,' Crane muttered, then softened his voice and even slipped his gun back in its holster. 'Just tell me, and if I like what I hear, you might live long enough to tell her, too.'

For long moments Truman hung his head, sighing, then straightened a last wrinkle from his collar and stood tall.

'It took me ten years to tame my land,' he murmured, his low tone suggesting he was talking to himself as much as to Crane. 'I redirected a river and cleared rocks using my own bare hands.' Truman raised his hands and stared at them as he turned them over. The hands were clean, but etched into the flesh were the calluses from years of manual work. 'But six years ago, my crops failed, cattle prices fell, and I was near to giving up. I threw my hopes into building a bridge and easing the passage to Sweetwater. I uprooted hundreds of trees for the wood. Then beneath one I found ... I found something.'

'A casket?' Crane whispered.

Truman glanced at Lincoln, then Seymour, then stared at Crane's feet.

'Yeah,' he murmured. 'I found a buried casket containing the gold you're looking for.'

'What did you do with it?' Crane snapped.

Truman shuffled his feet from side to side.

'I told nobody and kept it.'

'Yee-haw,' Rocco shouted, punching the air.

'And how much is left?' Crane croaked.

'All of it,' Truman said, his voice hurt. 'I resisted temptation and did nothing with it.'

With another joyous shout, Elwood and Wallace jumped on the spot and even hugged each other, then linked arms and jigged in a wild circle, taking turns to leap and click their heels together. Round and round they whirled, their whooping threatening to grow loud enough to be heard back in Sweetwater.

Crane stood back, grinning at their merriment. But when Rocco clapped a hand against a raised thigh with an infectious beat and Elwood started warbling a camp-fire song without recognizable words, or for that matter a recognizable tune, he raised his arms for quiet. Even then he joined his men and exchanged a round of back-slapping.

Crane chuckled, wending out from under Elwood and Wallace's congratu-latory huddle. He licked his lips, trying to suppress his grin, but when that failed, he patted Truman's shoulder.

'As I'm now in a right contented mood,' he said, 'I reckon I'll forgive you for finding our gold.'

'Yeah,' Rocco said, his voice the lightest Lincoln had heard. He strode across the trading post towards Truman. 'But only after you've given it back to us. So where is it now?'

Truman nodded. 'The gold is in my summer house, beyond the ridge.'

'A rectangular building,' Crane said, 'with wide doors at the front?'

'Yes.'

'Hot damn,' Elwood shouted, kicking the counter. 'I said that house was on the spot where Decker buried our gold.'

'You don't mean ... ' Crane murmured, slapping his forehead. 'You stored our gold in the exact same place you found it?'

'I did,' Truman said, his gaze still downcast. 'It is my folly, my shame, my ... I cannot explain it. I built that summer house for my wife in the most beautiful place in the valley. The views of the setting sun are so golden. I guess I wouldn't have wanted it in any other place.'

Crane and Wallace shared a pained glance and an exasperated sigh. Rocco even joined Elwood and patted his back, mumbling an apology for his earlier rough treatment of him.

'Now, if we're all finished being right apologetic,' Crane said, his former huge grin returning. 'You just have to come with us and we'll take that temptation away.'

'But I've told you where the gold is. You don't need me any more.'

'I just want to ensure you weren't lying.' Crane pointed to the door. 'And then, while we enjoy looking at our gold, you can enjoy looking at one of your golden sundowns.'

3

Lincoln leaned on the counter listening to Crane grunt a typical series of threats to Truman about what would happen if the gold wasn't in the summer house.

Throughout Crane's questioning of Truman, Lincoln had avoided provoking him into unnecessary violence and had done nothing to show that he was a lawman. He preferred to learn Crane's intentions, then pursue Crane when the outlaws had left and the innocent people in the trading post were no longer in danger.

So, when Crane finished threatening Truman, Lincoln stood back, waiting for him to leave, but Crane gathered Lincoln and Marvin, the stagecoach driver, around him. He searched them for hidden weapons, confiscating Marvin's gun, to Marvin's irritation, then pointed to the door.

To avoid word getting out, Crane ordered Seymour to accompany them, and the trading-post owner was wise enough not to argue.

Lincoln winced as the moment when the innocent bystanders were no longer in danger receded.

So, as the group headed out of the trading post, Lincoln resigned himself to a policy of avoiding provoking these men until he judged that it was the right moment to act. And as he'd heard of Decker Calhoun's raid twenty years ago, and had a sneaky admiration for a man who had carried out such a daring ambush while avoiding killing anyone, he reckoned he could probably avoid bloodshed.

Crane led them. Wallace and Elwood were at the back, carrying their spades. Rocco stalked at the side, aiming his gun in roving sweeps across their hostages.

During the fifteen minutes they had been in the trading post, the fog had thickened even more. From the doorway, the stagecoach was just an outline, although it was only twenty yards away. The blanket was cold and close, permeating deep into Lincoln's lungs with every damp breath.

One by one, the hostages piled into the stagecoach, but Crane held Lincoln back and directed him to join him and Marvin at the front.

'Why can't I sit with the others in the stagecoach?' Lincoln asked.

'Truman will do nothing foolish when Rocco's beside him,' Crane said. 'Seymour just wants to return to his trading post, and our driver just wants to return to his driving.'

'Yep,' Marvin said, jumping into his seat.

'But I ain't figured you out.' Crane looked Lincoln up and down, then pointed to the seat. 'You're a man who lied when I asked him his name, then says nothing when I confront the real Truman. I just don't trust you.'

Lincoln shrugged and without complaint sat on Marvin's right side. Crane sat on Marvin's left and pointed ahead.

Marvin yanked the reins and at a steady pace, the stagecoach trundled from the trading post.

Within ten rolls of the wheels, the fog filled in around them, hiding the trading post and leaving the stagecoach as the only object visible to Lincoln, creating the impression that they were the only people in the world. The fog even cut off all sounds other than the clop of the horses' hoofs and the creaking of the rolling stagecoach.

For the first hundred yards, Marvin kept a tight rein on the horses, their speed not much more than a man's walking pace.

'Go faster,' Crane muttered.

'I ain't going faster in weather like this,' Marvin said.

Crane snorted his irritation, which after a moment's thought, forced Marvin to stand and place a hand beside his mouth.

'What you doing?' Crane grunted.

Marvin glanced down at Crane. 'Hollering on ahead. Just in case somebody is riding towards us.'

'Sit.'

Marvin sighed, then fell back into his seat.

'Then don't blame me if we run into someone, break a wheel, then not reach that gold of yours.'

Crane snorted and slammed a firm hand on Marvin's shoulder.

'But I will. And you will go faster.'

While muttering under his breath, Marvin shook the reins and the horses speeded to at least a slow trot.

'What you so eager about?' Lincoln asked. 'You've waited twenty years to claim this gold. Another hour won't change anything.'

Crane glanced at Lincoln, then Marvin in turn.

'You two are mentioning our gold too often for my liking. Be quiet.'

Lincoln raised his hands, then leaned back against the stagecoach and peered ahead. Before him, the fog swirled and twined. Glimpses of shapes that might be trees, rocks, sometimes fences emerged, but by the time he'd decided what they were, the whiteness had stolen them from his view.

To avoid the fog inducing a headache he closed his eyes, but even with the blessed darkness, the fog pressed on him, closing off his world, forcing him to open his eyes and confront the blanket of whiteness.

A shape loomed ahead, solid and blocking the trail.

'Whoa!' he shouted, but Marvin was already pulling back on the reins.

As the stagecoach slowed, the shape emerged from the fog to reveal itself as a rider, standing sideways across the trail. He was still as the stagecoach lurched to a halt, stopping with a five-yard gap between him and the lead horses.

Held upright and perched on his right hip was a rifle.

Lincoln narrowed his eyes, but the

fog was too dense for him to discern the man's features.

Crane nudged Marvin into speaking.

'Howdy,' Marvin shouted. 'Fog is mighty tough for us travellers.'

The rider edged his horse a pace to the side, but still he blocked their route ahead.

At Lincoln's side, Crane slipped his gun from its holster and laid it across his lap, then nudged Marvin.

'Get that idiot to move,' he whispered.

'Be obliged if you'd let us pass,' Marvin shouted.

The rider stayed where he was. From under a lowered hat, he peered back, although Lincoln couldn't see his eyes.

'Give him ten seconds,' Crane murmured, 'then run him off the trail.'

Marvin nodded and wrapped his hands into the reins. He shook them enough to encourage the horses to edge a half-wheel forward.

But the rider sat impassive and firm-jawed.

Marvin edged forward a full wheel turn.

The horses balked as they closed on the man, but he kept a tight rein on his horse and stayed still.

But now that they were closer, Lincoln saw a hint of the man's eyes, which reflected the cold, fog-shrouded light. That was the only part of his features he could see. He leaned forward, his eyes narrowed to slits, searching for a reason why this man wasn't moving.

Then he saw it.

The man had a kerchief wrapped across his mouth.

'Ambush,' Lincoln murmured.

Crane swirled round to face him, but, as he opened his mouth to ask how he knew, more shapes loomed from the fog. A rider to the left, one to the right, then another riding straight towards them.

The men all had rifles, but held them high.

This was all the warning Marvin

needed and with a sharp shake of the reins, he urged his horses to head forward, but with the rider still standing on the trail, the lead horses reared and whinnied.

The man edged his horse back a pace but stayed before them, and the stagecoach horses lurched to the side. Marvin fought the horses a moment, then relented and let them veer from the trail, but kept them on a tight rein as they skimmed past the rider, then hurtled onwards in a short circle.

They trundled past the rider, but even though Crane turned his gun on him, the man sat impassive, his rifle pointing to the sky.

'Head back to the trail,' Crane snapped.

Marvin glanced left and right, peering at the flanking riders, who even as he stared, melted into the fog.

'Nope,' he said. 'I'm staying off the trail.'

'We can go faster on the trail. Off it, they can ambush us.'

'If that was an ambush, it was the oddest one I've ever seen.' Marvin shook the reins, lengthening out the tight circle. 'If they follow us, it'll prove whether it was one or not.'

'And then what?'

'Then you give me back my gun, because I ain't doing any defending without it.'

'That ain't what I . . . ' Crane sighed, then jumped to his feet and peered over the back of the stagecoach.

Lincoln glanced around the side of the stagecoach, but saw only the enclosing fog.

'Anybody?' Marvin asked.

'Nope,' Crane muttered, flopping back on to his seat. 'And you're still heading back to the trading post. Turn the stagecoach.'

'Quit whining. I'll look after the driving. You worry about the rest.' Marvin glanced at Crane but as Crane raised his gun to aim it at him, he winced. 'But once I know for sure they've gone, I'll head towards Sweetwater again.'

Lincoln turned and peered over his shoulder. He saw only the fog behind, but just as he was about to turn back, the outline of a rider emerged from the fog, then disappeared.

'They're still following us,' he said.

'At least we know they're after us,' Crane murmured. 'Now, speed up.'

'Going as fast as I can off the trail,' Marvin said, lurching from side to side as they thundered over a rock. He leaned forward in the seat with his eyes narrowed to slits.

'Then head back onto it and lose them in the fog.'

'The fog's spooking the horses. I'll never get much speed out of them, and those men can just follow the wheel tracks.'

Crane slapped his thigh, then jumped up to peer in all directions.

'The question you should ask is,' Lincoln said, 'are those men after you, or are they after the stagecoach?'

'Good point.' Crane dropped back into his seat and swirled round to face

Marvin. 'How long till we reach the trading post?'

'Three minutes.'

'Then stop.'

'I ain't stopping. We can't make a stand out here.'

'I don't intend to.'

Crane glared at Marvin until he pulled back on the reins, halting the horses. Even as they lurched to a halt, Crane was already dragging Marvin from the seat. He gestured for Lincoln to follow him, then dashed round the side and threw open the door for Rocco to jump down.

'What in tarnation are we doing?' Rocco muttered. 'And who are — ?'

'Be quiet,' Crane snapped. 'We're heading back to the trading post.'

'You can't be serious.'

'Those raiders are either after us or after the stagecoach. If it's us, we got no chance when we're in the open. If it's the stagecoach, they can have it.'

As Marvin whined, Rocco nodded and dragged Seymour and Truman from the stagecoach. They huddled and to Marvin's sullen directions headed off.

Within twenty paces, the stagecoach disappeared into the fog behind them, leaving them stranded in a sea of damp and cold air.

For another fifty or so paces they tramped, but as shouting and barked orders emerged from the fog behind them, presumably as the raiders found the deserted stagecoach, Crane hurried them on.

'This is ridiculous,' Elwood muttered, peering into the whiteness ahead. 'We should have got closer to the post.'

'We took our chance when they weren't near,' Crane said. 'And the post *is* close.'

In a huddle, they scurried. The raiders' shouting and orders drifted to them, the disorientating fog sometimes making their voices sound as if they came from ahead, then beside them, but Lincoln judged that they weren't closing on them.

By degrees, the ground became sandier, but the recent heavy frosts had frozen it, making it crunch with a crisp sound at every pace.

When Lincoln reckoned that they had travelled for the three minutes' worth that Marvin had promised, and still the post hadn't appeared, he glanced at Marvin.

Marvin returned a lip-biting glance that said he also thought they'd missed it.

They still scurried for another minute before Crane pulled everyone to a halt. He slammed a finger to his lips, then stood with his hands on his hips, peering in all directions. But the fog remained as impenetrable as ever and the ground remained just as rocky and unyielding of clues as to which direction they should take.

Crane grabbed Marvin. 'Which way now?'

With Rocco looming over him and cracking his knuckles, Marvin knelt and fingered the frozen dirt.

'I don't know,' he murmured, then looked up at Seymour, who joined him.

Seymour knelt. He peered at the nearest rock, but then stood and shrugged.

'Unless I see a landmark,' he said, 'I can't help.'

Rocco snorted. 'Can't or — '

A shout ripped through the air, silencing him, the words indistinct but seemingly coming from within yards of them.

With short gestures, Crane directed the four hostages to sit in a circle, five feet apart. Then he and his men backed to take the four points, and knelt facing outwards with their guns drawn, facing the impenetrable wall of fog.

For a full minute Lincoln sat, but as Crane continued to peer at the mist, he shuffled round to sit closer to Truman, staring at him until Truman returned a glance.

'We need to talk,' Lincoln whispered from the corner of his mouth.

Truman shook his head. 'We don't.

I'll get us out of this alive.'

'You won't. That ain't your job. But it is . . . ' An old cautionary instinct grabbed Lincoln, forcing him to look over his shoulder. Seymour and Marvin were both leaning back, clearly listening to the conversation. Without analysing why, Lincoln lowered his voice to the lowest of whispers so that only Truman could hear him. 'Say nothing, but I'm a US marshal.'

Truman blew out his cheeks.

'You travel with a man for two days,' he whispered, 'and he doesn't tell you that?'

'And I travelled with a man for two days and he didn't tell me about a stash of gold he'd found.'

'Point taken.'

'Now listen.' Lincoln raised his voice so that the others could hear. 'We'll all live through this, but only if you don't try to escape, or take on Crane's men, or do anything unexpected.'

Seymour and Marvin grunted their approval, but Truman shook his head.

'That won't help us.'

'It will. I'll do something unexpected at a time of my choosing or when the opportunity arises. But to succeed you need to tell me the truth.' Lincoln lowered his voice to the faintest of whispers again and placed his mouth over Truman's ear. 'So, tell me about the gold.'

Truman leaned back, sneering. 'I've told my story. There is no more.'

'When a man stares down the barrel of a gun, he'll say anything to stay alive.' Lincoln patted Truman's shoulder. 'But I don't have a gun on you.'

Truman glanced over his shoulder at the others, then sighed and leaned forward on his haunches to place his mouth over Lincoln's ear.

'I can't tell *you*,' he whispered.

'I understand. But if finding buried gold and doing nothing with it is a crime, it ain't a big one.' Lincoln patted Truman's shoulder. 'And I'll speak up for you.'

'Obliged. But what can I say to

convince you I told the truth?'

'Just look me in the eye and tell me what we'll find in your summer house. If the gold ain't there, it'll just change the way I deal with this.'

'The gold is in my summer house.' Truman placed his hand on his chest and stared into Lincoln's eyes. 'I swear that on my life, on my wife's life, on all our lives.'

Lincoln searched for any hint of deception on Truman's part, but Truman looked at him with firm conviction in his gaze.

'Then I believe you.'

Truman nodded. 'Now, tell me — what do you plan to do?'

'Don't worry. I've been in situations like this — '

'Quit talking, you two,' Rocco muttered, pacing from his point to confront Lincoln. He narrowed his eyes. 'I'm getting a big dislike of your face. If you annoy me again, I might think it ain't essential that you live long enough to see that summer house.'

'Rocco,' Crane muttered, looking over his shoulder, 'you ain't hurting anyone, and we are getting our gold. And we start doing that now. I reckon those raiders were after the stagecoach. So, they can have it, while we head to that summer house.'

Crane jumped to his feet and consulted his men as to which way they should go. Elwood peered at the sky, then pointed to the side and directed everyone to head that way.

'That ain't the right way,' Marvin said. He pointed over his shoulder in the exact opposite direction to the way that Elwood had pointed. 'That is.'

Crane tipped back his hat, his eyes flaring. 'You don't even know where the post is, so be quiet.'

'We want to head away from the stagecoach and find the trail,' Elwood said. He pointed to the sky. 'It's lighter up there, so the sun is that way and at this time of day, it's in the south. I reckon we should reach the trail in two minutes.'

Elwood stared at Marvin with his eyebrows raised until he nodded. Then Crane shepherded everyone into a group. He muttered firm orders to the hostages to stay quiet, then took the lead with Elwood at his side and Rocco and Wallace walking behind the hostages.

At a steady pace, they headed in the direction Elwood had indicated.

For five minutes they shuffled forward, silence surrounding them and no landmarks appearing to confirm whether they were heading in the right direction or steering a straight course.

Then, from out of the swirling fog ahead, a shape appeared, dark and angular.

Crane halted everyone and edged forward three more paces. He hung his head a moment, then beckoned everyone to approach.

Lincoln joined him, peering ahead at the shape. He winced.

The shape was the stagecoach.

4

Beside the stagecoach, Crane ordered the group to halt. He peered around. The raiders had gone and so had the horses.

'Hot damn but they didn't have to take my horses,' Marvin whined, slapping his hat against his thigh.

Seymour snorted. 'We're stranded, a gang of jailbirds are holding us hostage, and another group of raiders are harassing us. And all you care about is your horses.'

'Yeah,' Marvin said, shrugging.

'Anything stolen?' Crane asked.

Marvin nodded. 'Yeah. They took everything and ran off my horses.'

'But did they take anything valuable?'

'My horses.'

'Anything *else* valuable?'

Marvin glanced up at the stagecoach roof. 'I was delivering a whole heap of bags to Sweetwater. I guess there could have been valuables in them. They didn't take your spades, mind.'

'So, at least we know for sure that they weren't looking for us,' Crane mused, then motioned for Rocco to circle the stagecoach, twenty-five yards out, the maximum distance that kept him in view.

When Rocco returned and confirmed that he hadn't seen or heard the raiders, Crane ordered the hostages to stand by the stagecoach, leaving Wallace to guard them while he considered his options with Elwood and Rocco.

'Now that we know we're safe,' Rocco said, 'we should head to that summer house again.'

Perhaps, but as your suggestions are usually wrong . . . ' Crane glanced at Elwood.

'I reckon we can walk all day,' Elwood said, gesturing all around him at the blanket of fog. 'But until this fog lifts, we got no way of knowing for sure if we're heading in the right direction.'

'Unless you get it right,' Rocco grunted, 'and we find the trail.'

'And then it's three, maybe four miles to the summer house. And that'll take more than an hour, and — '

'Quit whining,' Crane grunted. 'I've had enough of waiting, too. And I know you can find the trail.'

Crane glared at Elwood, receiving a nod, then held his hand to the side, letting him choose his direction.

With Crane's confidence in him swelling his chest, Elwood hunkered down beside a sprawl of hoof prints and sniffed the air. He shrugged, then pointed at the slight indentation the wheels had made in the frozen ground.

'We'll follow the tracks first,' he said. 'Then we'll veer to the left and reach the trail more quickly.'

Crane nodded and told Elwood to fetch a spade from the stagecoach. Then he placed Truman and Lincoln at the flanking positions ten yards to his left and right and a pace ahead of him so that he could watch them both.

They set off with everyone else trailing in a line behind him and with Rocco at the rear.

As they veered from the wheel tracks, Crane ordered Elwood to stop and at intervals of twenty paces, use his spade to gouge a furrow, which pointed back towards the stagecoach.

For five minutes they walked at a steady pace, then Elwood raised a hand, halting them.

With a finger to his lips, Crane swirled round and gestured for the others to halt, while Elwood craned his neck with his right ear held high, his studious gaze making an obvious show of his listening.

For a full minute Crane humoured Elwood, then stalked to his side and slapped a hand on his shoulder.

'I can't hear anything,' he murmured.

'Be quiet,' Elwood whispered. 'I can.'

Crane glanced at Lincoln, who shrugged, but then matched Elwood's posture, even cupping his ear as he listened.

Crane sighed, then joined them in the strained listening. With everyone standing rigid and with the absence of even the lightest breath of a breeze, total silence surrounded them, the lack of sound as thick and cloying as the constrained vision in their white prison.

But then a horse whinnied.

Crane nodded to Elwood who flashed a smile back.

'Seems we won't have to walk,' Elwood said, slapping his thigh. 'We can still go to the summer house in Marvin's stagecoach.'

Crane snorted. 'You offering to drag it there?'

'Nope. They may have ran off the horses, but horse-thieving is a mighty serious offence for little reward. I reckon they've had enough sense to abandon them and just keep everything else.'

The whinny came again, then the clop of hoofs. And the sounds were closing.

Elwood winced and shuffled back a pace.

Crane grabbed his elbow and dragged him towards the direction of the whinnying horse.

'The horse is that way,' he whispered, pointing forward.

'That ain't the problem,' Elwood said with a gulp. 'This horse has a rider.'

With a snap of his wrist, Crane released his grip of Elwood's arm.

He gestured to everyone to head back to the stagecoach, and the group paced backwards, but then the sounds came — a horse clopping, leather creaking, and Lincoln reckoned it just had to be one of the raiders.

And from the sound of it, he was only yards away.

Then a rider appeared ahead, faint and spectral, tendrils of fog wreathing his form, and he was heading straight at them.

Crane didn't need to deliver any more warnings as everyone turned and dashed back towards the stagecoach. At a trot they reached the first gouged mark in the earth, then, as one, thrust their heads down and hurtled for the second marking.

Lincoln glanced over his shoulder. The man had disappeared back into the fog, but then appeared again only to disappear a moment later.

Rocco danced round, still running, but fell back as he arced his gun up to fire when the rider next appeared.

'Don't,' Crane muttered. 'Firing will tell the rest where we are.'

Rocco grunted, then slammed his gun back in its holster and concentrated on running.

They scurried past the third and fourth markings.

Lincoln reckoned Elwood must have marked out at least twenty and a man couldn't outrun a horse over that distance, but every time he looked back, their pursuer was just on the edge of his vision.

'What in tarnation is he doing?' Rocco whined.

Elwood slowed his running to a trot and fell back.

'He's toying with us,' he said. 'That's what he's doing.'

Crane ran on for another few paces, then slowed to let Elwood join him. Lincoln slowed, too, and glanced over his shoulder, but still the man stayed back so that the fog blurred his form.

Crane gestured for everyone else to stop, then swung to a halt and glared at the faint form of the rider with his hands on his hips.

Two paces on, the rider also halted, closer than before so that his form stood out in stark relief against the white blanket behind. From under a lowered hat, he stared at Crane. A kerchief still hid his lower features and his rifle rested on his hip, pointing straight up.

With slow paces he backed a horse length, letting the fog blur his form again.

'This just ain't right,' Crane murmured. 'Why doesn't he do something?'

Elwood sighed. 'I reckon we should just be grateful that he ain't and head back to the stagecoach.'

'I ain't,' Rocco muttered, pacing to Crane's side. 'I'm getting a reaction if it's the last thing I do.'

Rocco ripped his gun from its holster and standing sideways sighted the man down the barrel.

'Don't,' Crane said. 'You'll get us killed.'

Rocco snorted and swung round to face the rider, but he let his gun drop to aim downwards and took deep calming breaths.

The rider kept his rifle pointed high.

Crane stared at the impassive raider, but then he glanced at Rocco and nodded. With a huge grin, Rocco swung his gun up, staring at the rider as he searched for a hint that he was going to react.

But the rifle stayed high and the rider impassive.

Rocco swung his gun to the side, aiming at a boulder ten feet away then arced the gun barrel around the rider's form.

But still the rider stayed still.

With his other hand, Rocco rubbed the sweat from his brow, then inched his gun in towards the man.

The horse tossed its head, but with a calming hand the rider stilled it.

'Do something, damn you,' Rocco roared. He swung his gun up and deliberately fired high.

The gunshot ripped through the silence.

The man stayed a moment, then backed away to fade into the fog.

'Hot damn but you got a reaction,' Crane said. 'And a good one.'

'It wasn't,' Lincoln whispered. 'That gunshot just told everyone exactly where we are.'

'And they're coming,' Elwood murmured, his eyes wide.

Lincoln strained to hear what had scared Elwood. But although he heard only the clop of hoofs as the horse backed from them, Crane nodded and turned, then scurried for the next marking on the ground, encouraging everyone to join him.

With their hostages herded into the centre of the group, the men ran in a ragged circle, but by the time they'd passed another three markings, Lincoln heard the pursuers. He had seen at least six men before, and from the clatter of the cascading hoofs, all of them were closing on them.

The sounds came from behind, the left, the right, as they converged on them.

Lincoln darted his gaze around, searching for his first glimpse of the riders, but his vision washed over the blanket of endless whiteness that surrounded him.

'How many more to the stagecoach?' Elwood asked as they dashed over another marking.

'Eight,' Crane shouted, 'maybe less.'

A rider loomed to the left, then a second, then one to the right.

As Crane fired a speculative shot over his shoulder, Lincoln thrust his head down and scampered headlong into the fog heedless of where his feet landed. The group spread, the youngest, Rocco, gaining the front, and the oldest, Elwood, falling back.

Lincoln counted four more markings, by which time the men were flanking them.

Hoofbeats thundered around them. And if they wanted to, they could have blasted the group to oblivion in a moment. But they rode with calm precision, a horse length apart and possibly shepherding them back to the stagecoach.

Crane danced round in a circle as he ran, appraising their pursuers, but as all of them had their rifles held high, he thrust his gun back in its holster.

Then ahead, the outline of the stagecoach appeared. Rocco and Wallace reached it first and immediately knelt, then trained their guns ahead. Lincoln reached the stagecoach next, but Wallace pushed him inside, closely followed by the other hostages, then joined Rocco in kneeling.

Through the stagecoach window

Lincoln watched Crane speed, his feet pounding into the earth and his head thrust forward.

'Open fire when I give the order,' Crane shouted, then threw himself to the ground to slide towards the stagecoach, coming to a halt beside the back wheel.

'Fire at what?' Rocco muttered.

Crane rolled to his side to lie beside Rocco and peer into the fog.

The riders had gone.

He rolled out from under the stagecoach and jumped to his feet, then stomped ten paces, but the riders hadn't followed them.

Fifteen yards before the stagecoach, Elwood slowed to a halt, his face bright red. He dropped his spade and slammed his hands on his knees as he regained his breath.

Crane pointed into the fog.

'Can you hear them?' he shouted.

'Not over . . . not over . . . ' Elwood wheezed a great gasp of air. 'Not over my breathing.'

'Then stop breathing and listen.' Crane aimed his gun at Elwood's chest for emphasis.

Elwood took a deep breath and peered into the fog, then raised a hand for quiet.

'They're close,' he said, gasping and pointing to the right. 'Maybe fifty yards that way.'

Crane swung round to face the direction Elwood was pointing.

'We're here,' he roared. 'Come and get us.'

The fog swallowed his voice, giving no hint as to whether it would carry to the riders.

'Who are you?' Crane blasted a speculative shot into the fog. 'What do you want?' Crane stormed forward and kicked at the earth. 'Why are you after us?'

Crane stood, waiting for an answer — probably any answer — but the fog just swirled around him. With his head down, he shuffled back to the stage-coach, his gun held low and his jaw set firm enough to grind his teeth to dust.

'I can't stand much more of this,' Rocco muttered, wiping sweat from his brow. 'Why don't they just come?'

'I got no idea,' Crane grunted, and kicked a stone. 'What sort of men hold their fire for this long?'

'You got a point,' Lincoln shouted.

Crane swirled round to face him. 'You reckon you know the answer?'

'Nope.' Lincoln shrugged, but then stepped down from the stagecoach and raised a finger. 'But if you're desperate to know the answer, I reckon I can find it out.'

'How?'

Lincoln strode three slow paces and peered around at the blanket of whiteness, then hunkered down to finger the frozen ground.

'I'm beginning to understand the lie of the land. If those men are playing a waiting game, I reckon I can use that time to scout around. In this fog I can stay hidden and see how many men we're up against and who they are.'

Crane snorted. 'You're going nowhere.'

Lincoln held his hands wide. 'You have to trust me.'

'I ain't ever doing that.'

Lincoln pointed at the stagecoach. 'Crane, you got four hostages and four men to guard them, and you got maybe six men waiting to kill you.'

'Trusting you won't change the odds.'

'It won't, but . . . ' Lincoln beckoned Crane to walk from the stagecoach and after a steady rub of his chin, Crane paced to his side.

'Let's hear it.'

'As you've said — Seymour's too scared to try anything. Marvin and Truman are just waiting for this to end. I'm the only one you ain't figured out yet, so you're spending as much time watching me as looking out for those raiders. If I join you, that's one more of you and one more chance of you taking on our opponents.'

'That's mighty fine reasoning. But why do you want to join us?'

'I want to live.' Lincoln grinned. 'And if you want, I can name another fifty thousand reasons.'

'We spent twenty years rotting in Barton jail,' Rocco shouted, storming from the stagecoach and barging Crane aside in his eagerness to confront Lincoln. 'We ain't giving up a share to nobody.'

Lincoln stood his ground. 'Fifty thousand dollars is an awful lot of money. I reckon you can spare some of it.'

'That's enough, Rocco,' Crane snapped, flashing Rocco a harsh glare that made him back up a pace. He lowered his head a moment, then shrugged. 'But whenever my hot-headed friend thinks something is a bad idea, it usually makes me think it is. You can go. Find out who they are, and you'll get a nice return.'

'Hey,' Rocco muttered, squaring up to Crane. 'We didn't agree to that.'

'We didn't. But it is what I want.'

Rocco glared at Crane, his fists opening and closing, but then with an angry slap of a fist against his thigh, he turned and stalked back to the stagecoach, muttering to himself.

Crane watched him until he joined Wallace and Elwood beside the stagecoach, then turned to Lincoln and pointed into the fog.

Lincoln tipped his hat, then with long paces, returned to the stagecoach.

He placed his back against the stagecoach and peered into the sky, selecting the brightest point, then paced towards it.

On the tenth pace, he gouged out a mark in the ground with his heel, then paced on. When he'd counted another ten paces, he glanced over his shoulder to confirm that the stagecoach had disappeared into the fog.

Lincoln smiled and made an abrupt left turn.

5

Crane had asked what sort of men held their fire when ambushing.

Only at that moment did Lincoln realize, with embarrassment, what ought to have been obvious to him the moment the raiders had first appeared.

He didn't know for sure why they were acting the way they were or what they planned to achieve with their delaying tactics.

But now he reckoned he knew who they were.

And Lincoln backed his hunches.

So, for twenty paces he walked, then stopped and peered around until he found the markings Elwood had made earlier. He followed these, heading away from the stagecoach, but as he passed each marking, he reduced the stealth of his walking.

He clumped his feet and batted his

hands against his legs, trying to attract their tormentors' attention while falling short of making a noise that was loud enough for Crane to hear back at the stagecoach.

He expected the men to close on him quickly but to his surprise, he reached Elwood's final marking without them approaching.

So there, he stopped.

The men would have formed a base near to the stagecoach — that's what Lincoln would have done — but in the fog he had little chance of finding it. So he waited, presuming that the systematic sweeps the men must be carrying out, while keeping each other in sight, would soon find him.

Sure enough, after ten minutes of waiting, hoofbeats clumped nearby. Then a rider emerged from the fog and immediately pulled back on the reins, halting just on the edge of Lincoln's vision.

This time, because Lincoln was looking for it, he saw the man gesture before he halted, presumably signalling to his companions who were too far back in the fog for Lincoln to see them.

Lincoln raised his hands to shoulder level, then turned on the spot, showing that he wasn't packing a gun, then patted his jacket.

The rider merely stared at him.

Lincoln strode a long pace, then lowered his hands to his side and stood tall.

'I want to talk,' he said, then strode another pace.

The rider backed his horse a pace.

'We could play this game all day,' Lincoln said, 'but unless you want to back all the way to Sweetwater, I'd stop and listen to me.'

He paced another stride, but the man backed away again.

'You got no reason to avoid me,' Lincoln said. He stopped and set his hands on his hips. '*Deputy.*'

The rider sat impassive, but Lincoln reckoned he detected a slight movement from him, perhaps his shoulders slumping a mite. Then the man advanced his horse a pace.

Lincoln smiled. 'Seems I got your attention. I ain't packing a gun. And I ain't no threat. I just want to talk to the marshal.'

The rider advanced another pace so that Lincoln could see his eyes, but they were blank and he still kept his kerchief over his nose and mouth. Then he turned his horse to the side and pointed ahead with his rifle.

Lincoln nodded and headed in the direction that the rifle was pointing. As he passed the rider, he kept his gaze set forward, but within five paces, he heard the steady clop of hoofs as the horse followed him.

From the corner of his eye, he glanced to the side to see that two other men were now flanking him and, just as they had shepherded the group back to the stagecoach earlier, they left a clear space ahead.

Lincoln counted 200 paces. Then, from out of the fog, shapes appeared ahead. Within five more paces, the shapes resolved into four men who were sitting on the ground facing each other.

The largest of the men jumped to his feet and paced round to face Lincoln. Two men glared up at him, but remained sitting.

But the other man sat with his knees drawn up to his chin, his head hanging and his bony shoulders slumped. In the murky light, Lincoln couldn't tell for sure but this man was probably older than the others and might have had chains around his wrists.

Behind these men were the horses that they'd taken from the stagecoach and a heap of bags, which Lincoln now reckoned they'd stolen to present the illusion of a raid.

Lincoln tore his gaze away from his appraisal of the encampment and stopped five paces from the large man. He tipped his hat.

'Howdy, Marshal,' he said.

The man's right eye twitched. 'An interesting guess.'

Lincoln smiled. 'And I'm mighty relieved to get a response from you people. I was getting to think you were all dumb. But I'm right, ain't I?'

'We're lawmen,' the marshal snorted, and glanced over Lincoln's shoulder at the rider who had found him. 'I told you not to capture them.'

'I didn't,' the rider said, his voice distorted through the kerchief. He drew his horse to stand alongside Lincoln. 'He gave himself up.'

'Still didn't want no prisoners.' The marshal shrugged, but then stood to the side and stared back at the older man. 'You like meeting your old friend?'

The old man unfurled his legs from his chest, an action that confirmed to Lincoln that he *was* wearing chains, then looked up at Lincoln, his eyes tired and blank.

'Don't know him,' he murmured, then returned to staring at his knees.

The marshal swirled round to face Lincoln.

'Then who are you?'

Lincoln folded his arms and set his feet in a firm stance. 'I'm Lincoln Hawk, another US marshal.'

'Ain't heard of you.'

'But I've heard of you. You're Marshal Zandana, the lawman who rounded up the Calhoun gang.' Lincoln pointed at the older man. 'And the man sitting over there is Decker Calhoun.'

The marshal sneered. 'You've done yourself some thinking.'

'I have. You're the only man who'd bother to follow Crane. You hoped he'd lead you to the gold, but you didn't expect him to take hostages. Then you had to stay close enough to take him if he tried anything, while avoiding spooking him too much or he might kill someone.'

'You figured out some of my plans, but not all of them.' The marshal smiled, but the lips were thin and harsh. 'But now that you're here, you can help me fill in the gaps. Has Crane got the gold yet?'

'Nope.' Lincoln glanced around the

arc of deputies. All of them glared back from under lowered hats, their eyes blank, kerchiefs still hiding the bottom halves of their faces. 'But you already knew that. You're giving Crane enough leeway to go for it.'

'So where is the gold?'

Lincoln opened his mouth to reply, but that old cautionary instinct that had rumbled earlier seized his guts and forced him to reply with a shrug.

'I don't know.'

'Then why has Crane kidnapped those people?'

'Crane's keeping his plans to himself. Truman Garner is a rich man. So, I reckon he's given up on finding the gold and has settled for whatever he can shake out of Truman.'

'And you escaped, did you, *Marshal* Lincoln Hawk?'

'I didn't. Crane let me go to scout around.'

'Crane let one of his hostages go! And a lawman at that.' Zandana snorted. 'Even Crane ain't that stupid.'

'He doesn't know I'm a lawman, just like he ain't figured out that you are either. But I've earned his trust. So, once we've agreed on how we can work together, I can return and help you to free the hostages.'

Zandana sneered. 'We ain't agreeing anything. And you are going nowhere.'

'But I can help you.'

Zandana swaggered towards Lincoln until he stood a pace before him. He smirked when he discovered that they shared the same eye-line.

'You got the wrong idea about your role here. There's only one thing you can do for me.'

Lincoln set his hands on his hips. 'And what's that?'

Zandana grinned and glanced at each of his deputies in turn, but then swirled back and thundered a right cross into Lincoln's cheek that sent him sprawling.

Lincoln's head cracked against the hard ground. He shook his head then, with shaking arms, tried to rise, but his vision swirled and he fell back.

Zandana loomed over him. 'You can be quiet. That's what you can do. I've run out of patience and I ain't playing waiting games no more.'

Zandana dragged Lincoln to his feet and pushed him in the general direction of the stagecoach.

With grogginess still befuddling his mind, Lincoln wheeled to a halt, then staggered round to face Zandana.

'I'm a lawman. I can help you.'

'You're no lawman and you're no help.' Zandana pointed over Lincoln's shoulder. 'And as I ain't looking for no talking back, one more word from you and I'll chain you up like Calhoun. Now move.'

Lincoln raised his hands and retreated, and with that acquiescence, Zandana directed his deputies to remove their kerchiefs and head out.

As the deputies collected the stagecoach horses, Zandana grabbed Decker's chain and yanked him to his feet, then mounted his horse and with

Decker running along beside him, led him from the camp.

As he scurried past, Decker glanced at Lincoln and shook his head, a mixture of amusement and sorrow in his eyes.

Lincoln rubbed the back of his head, feeling for a bruise, but one of the trailing deputies chivvied him along. So, at a trot, he hurried after Decker and Zandana.

He counted his paces and, although he didn't pass the markings Crane had made, he was able to judge the distance back.

At around a hundred yards away from the stagecoach, Zandana called everyone to a halt and placed a finger to his lips. He saved a harsh glare and finger drawn across his throat for Lincoln.

As Lincoln raised his hands and edged to his side to join Decker, two deputies paced ahead, twenty yards apart, and within moments, disappeared into the fog.

Lincoln braced himself for Crane's panicked gunfire, but when the deputies emerged from the fog, they gestured frantically for Zandana and the others to join them.

In a bunch, the deputies broke into a trot and, suspecting what he'd see, Lincoln hurried to keep up.

Sure enough, when the stagecoach appeared, Crane had deserted it.

Zandana leapt down from his horse and stormed around the stagecoach. He even leapt inside and hurled two spades through the windows, then stalked down to confront Lincoln.

'Now, there was me all ready to believe you really were a lawman.' Zandana gestured back at the stagecoach. 'Then you go and do this.'

Lincoln shrugged. 'I did nothing. Crane's just left.'

'And you ain't a decoy to distract us while he escaped?'

'From the look of things, that's what he did, but I didn't know he planned to do that.'

'And I reckon you did.' Zandana raised his fist and advanced a long pace on Lincoln. 'And now, I'll beat the rest of the story out of you.'

6

'The fog's lifting,' Elwood shouted. He halted his progress along the ridge and put a hand to his brow, then nodded. 'Yep. I *can* see further.'

'Be quiet,' Crane murmured, as he drew alongside, but as Elwood continued to peer down the slope, he glanced around. 'But I guess you're right. The fog *is* going.'

Although Crane had originally decided that the raiders wanted the valuables on the stagecoach, he'd changed his opinion and accepted that they wanted them. Or more specifically, that they wanted the gold.

So, when Lincoln had left to scout around, Crane guessed that they'd find him a lot faster than he'd find them. And as the raiders couldn't be in two places at once, that meant Lincoln had earned him a distraction.

The ridge to which they had headed earlier in the week to find their gold had stretched for miles in either direction. They'd followed it to find the trading post, becoming mired in the fog only when they'd dropped to a lower level to await Truman's arrival.

To start making significant progress, Crane reckoned they had to reach that ridge instead of the trail and free themselves of the fog that was so hamstringing their progress.

So, with Marvin's help, Elwood had orientated himself, then headed straight for the ridge.

This time, they'd steered a straight enough course, not even needing to backtrack and use the markings Elwood and Wallace had gouged into the earth, and they'd reached higher ground within five minutes.

And with that encouragement, they'd headed uphill.

Within ten minutes of leaving the trail, the incline had grown and as Elwood had just confirmed, their visibility range had grown, too. This meant that the raiders would also be able to see them from further away, but Crane fancied his chances in the open when they couldn't torment him from behind the veil of fog.

Crane encouraged everyone to hurry and, within another ten minutes, they were high enough to increase their range of visibility to almost a quarter-mile.

Confident now that this strategy was the right one, they headed south, following the contours of the ridge.

Crane took the lead, Rocco stayed at the back and Elwood and Wallace flanked their hostages.

With every passing minute, Marvin gained a more cheerful mood, repeatedly stating that a return to his previous driving work was imminent — provided he could find his horses.

But Seymour continued to grumble about the inappropriateness of having to walk so far.

Only Truman was sullen and quiet,

but whether that was from fear of what they would find when they reached the summer house, Crane didn't like to ponder too much.

Every hundred yards or so, Crane glanced down the side of the ridge at the blanket of fog below, expecting that at any moment the raiders would emerge.

But the white envelope remained unbroken.

The ground was slick and pebble-strewn, slowing their speed and Rocco became increasingly twitchy, his frequent stopping to aim down at imaginary foes emerging from the fog slowing them even more.

But even with these distractions, they made reasonable time.

After less than an hour's walking, Elwood judged that they had reached the spot where only four days ago they had first discovered the cleared forest.

So there, they crested the ridge and peered down the other side.

The late winter sun hadn't burnt off

enough of the fog for the summer house to be clear of its embrace yet. So, it was with a combination of excitement and trepidation that Crane directed everyone to head to a lower level.

Ten minutes of sliding and gingerly finding a route down the slope later, the fog closed in again, although to Crane's relief it wasn't as thick as it had been around the trading post.

Strangely, his first sight of the summer house emerging from the fog ahead only helped to darken his mood.

Elwood though whooped and his good humour dragged a low cheer from Rocco and Wallace.

Crane firmed his jaw and didn't join in the celebrations. Instead, he slapped Truman's shoulder with the back of his hand, halting him.

'I've waited a long time to claim our gold,' he said, keeping his voice as level as he could. 'And all the distractions today haven't helped my patience. So, I ask you for the last time — where is the gold?'

Truman faced him and with a firm arm, pointed down the slope.

'The gold is in my summer house.'

For long moments Crane stared at Truman, searching his unmoving eyes, then nodded and set off down the slope to the house.

'And I hope for your sake that it is,' he murmured.

Crane broke into a run and was the first to reach the house, but he stopped on the porch to appraise the building.

The squat adobe-walled summer house was about twenty feet by thirty feet.

A twin set of doors faced west, presumably so that Truman and his wife could enjoy watching their golden sundowns. Through these large, open doors he saw that two rooms were within, an open doorway connecting them.

At the back, small windows in each room faced east.

Crane paced through the doors and once inside, he was still as cold as he had been outside. He could even see his own breath pluming out from his mouth and it was as thick as the fog that had plagued them all day.

Propped against the back wall were random items of furniture — four chairs, a table, a chest.

Aside from these stark offerings, the room was bare, the floor just dirt, the walls unadorned.

Crane beckoned the others to follow him in and, in a line, the hostages entered the building, followed by his men. To Crane's directions the hostages stood along the back wall beside the window.

Crane ran his gaze along the furniture, then turned to Truman and raised his eyebrows.

'Our gold, *now*,' he said, trying to keep his voice calm, but hearing it emerge gruff and harsh.

'I can't give it you *now*.' Truman pointed through the doorway into the second room. 'I reburied it.'

'You reburied it,' Crane intoned, his

guts rumbling as the moment he reclaimed his gold receded again.

'Yeah.'

'And why didn't you mention that?' Rocco snapped. 'We only brought the spades with us to mark our progress.'

'I just didn't think that . . . ' Truman lowered his head as Rocco grunted a sharp oath, then shrugged his jacket straight and looked around the room. Then he paced to the corner.

With deliberately slow and long paces, he walked beside the side wall, counting to three, then scuffed that position with his heel. He continued to the other corner, counting four paces, then returned to his mark. He adjusted the mark a half-pace to signify the exact centre of the wall, then placed his back to the wall so that he faced the doorway to the second room.

Crane backed Elwood and Rocco out of his way and Truman walked from the wall with slow paces.

On the count of five paces, Truman reached the doorway to the second room and stopped, nodded, then set off again, counting three paces. He dug his heel in the ground, marking a small circle, then continued to the end wall, counting a further three paces.

Then, with his hands held out, he turned and faced Crane through the doorway.

'That's it,' he said, pointing at his heel mark. 'Eight paces from the side wall, right in the centre of the side room.'

Crane nodded as he strode into the doorway. 'And that's where you reburied our gold, no tricks?'

Truman flashed a smile. 'Yeah, no tricks. You'll find it in the exact same place Decker Calhoun buried it.'

'That just ain't fair,' Elwood whined. 'He even used the same hole.'

Truman shrugged. 'I had no intention of using the gold and it was just too much trouble to dig another one.'

Crane glanced over his shoulder at Elwood. 'You reckon that sounds right?'

Elwood wandered to the window,

shaking his head, and peered outside then returned, shrugging.

'When he cleared the trees, he removed most of the landmarks Decker mentioned. I got no way of knowing for sure whether this is the right place or not.'

Crane nodded and turned back to Truman. 'Then I have to trust you.' Crane pointed a firm finger at Truman. 'But if you're lying . . . '

'I ain't.'

Crane continued to point at Truman, giving him one last chance to change his story. But when Truman just returned his glare and even set his hands on his hips, Crane exchanged a pained glance with Rocco, then lowered his hand and forced a grim smile.

'How deep, then?'

'Slightly deeper than I found it. Four foot, maybe five.'

Crane stood aside and set Rocco and Wallace to digging, then directed his hostages into the adjoining room.

With his heel Rocco scraped a larger

circle, about four feet across, then flat-shovelled the topmost dirt away. Then he and Wallace started digging, slamming their spades down from chest height, then scraping away the earth they'd prised out. For two minutes they worked, the cussing from Rocco and Wallace worsening with each slam of their spades.

Then Wallace screeched and hurled his spade to the ground.

'What's wrong?' Crane shouted, peering through the doorway.

'The ground's frozen,' Wallace whined, wringing his hand. 'It's as hard as rock.'

'Yeah,' Rocco muttered, crashing his spade down. The spade bounced from the ground with a dull clang. He watched it rattle to a halt, then stormed into the doorway to confront Crane. 'If our gold's down there, we ain't ever getting to it.'

7

'Had enough?' Zandana muttered, lowering his fist.

Flat on his back, Lincoln clutched his jaw, but he still stared defiantly up at Zandana.

'You're a lawman,' he said, keeping his voice low despite the anger that was ripping through his guts. 'You can't mistreat your prisoners.'

'And that's where you're wrong. You ain't even earned the right to be a prisoner yet.' Zandana flexed his fist and advanced a long pace to loom over Lincoln. 'And I reckon you've still got too much fight left in you.'

With a large hand, Zandana hauled Lincoln to his feet and thundered a blow into his guts that sent him stumbling back and to his knees.

Lincoln flexed his chest, fighting down the burst of nausea that'd hit him, then rolled on his side and to his haunches. He stared at the ground, taking deep breaths as he forced down the anger that had grabbed him the moment Zandana had denied his story. But when his efforts failed, he leapt to his feet and with a huge roar, charged Zandana.

He hit him full in the chest with his shoulder and knocked him back three paces before Zandana tumbled on his back. Zandana hit the ground heavily, Lincoln landing on top of him, but he still bucked Lincoln from him. Lincoln though had a firm grip of Zandana's shoulders and the two men rolled to the side, each trying to wrestle the other man down.

Lincoln flexed his shoulders, straining to force Zandana on to his back, but Zandana matched his actions, resisting him, so with a snap of his wrists, Lincoln broke his hold and hurled a flailing blow at Zandana's face.

At the last moment, Zandana ripped his head back and the blow merely skimmed off his forehead, but Lincoln followed through with a firmer slug to his exposed cheek. Zandana shrugged it off, his eyes blazing as he hurled up a forearm and deflected Lincoln's next punch. Then he thrust out the forearm, trying to bundle Lincoln away, but Lincoln let the blow hit him and rolled away.

Lincoln continued the roll until he was well out of Zandana's reach, then leapt to his feet and stood hunched with his hands open and spread, and his feet planted in a firm stance.

'If I have to knock sense into you, I will,' he muttered. 'But one way or another, Zandana, you'll listen to me.'

Zandana rolled to his haunches and appraised Lincoln's stance with an arrogant gleam in his eyes. 'The only one getting sense knocked into them is you,' he grunted.

Zandana matched Lincoln's stance, then stalked towards him, his gait light for such a huge man. But just out of Lincoln's reach, he edged to the side, forcing Lincoln to wheel to keep facing him.

Zandana completed a half-circle. Then, just as he raised his foot for another step, he stormed in and hurled his arms around Lincoln in a huge bear-hug. Lincoln's ribs creaked and protested, but he stood his ground and wrapped his arms around his adversary, then locked them behind Zandana's back and with his own back flexed, attempted to close his arms.

In his grip, Zandana squirmed and with a long exhalation of air, the pressure around Lincoln's chest lessened. With renewed vigour, Lincoln thrust in his elbows, trying to squeeze Zandana into submission.

Zandana flexed his chest, but failed to halt Lincoln's rib-crunching progress. He kicked out, trying to knock Lincoln's legs from under him, but Lincoln had a wide and solid grip on the ground.

Zandana pulled his head back so that Lincoln could see the veins popping out on his forehead, his eyes wide and blazing. But then he jerked his head forward, his mouth open and his teeth bared, and seeing what he intended to do, Lincoln darted his own head back and released his grip.

Zandana's attempted ear-biting failed as his teeth clattered together on air.

Free now, Zandana staggered forward, momentarily off-balance and, using this advantage, Lincoln hurled a long, round-armed punch that crunched into the point of his chin and snapped his head back. Then he followed through with a flurry of blows to the chest and guts that knocked Zandana on his back, ploughing him through four feet of dirt before he came to a halt.

'You ready to listen?' Lincoln roared, standing over Zandana with his fists raised.

Zandana snorted. With the back of his left hand, he wiped a dribble of blood from his bottom lip, then hurled his right hand to his holster.

Lincoln kicked out, his flailing boot catching Zandana's arm and knocking it from his gun, but Zandana shuffled back along the ground and, as he reached for his gun again, Lincoln hurled himself on top of him.

With his right arm strained and taut, he pressed Zandana into the dirt and with his left hand, batted Zandana's hand away from his holster. As Zandana floundered, Lincoln released his grip and swung down to rip the gun from its holster himself. In a lithe action, he fell away, rolling over a shoulder to come to a halt on one knee with the gun cocked and aimed at Zandana's head.

Zandana glared down the barrel of the gun.

'You ain't no lawman,' he muttered, 'and you've just proved everything I reckoned I knew about you.'

'I haven't.' Lincoln firmed his gun hand. 'And as this is the only way I could make you listen, you gave me no choice. Now listen, damn you!'

'Do I look like I want to listen?' Zandana glanced away from the gun to look at the surrounding deputies. 'Do any of us look like we'll listen to a man who has a gun on a marshal?'

Lincoln glanced around the arc of uncompromising deputies facing him. Every man glared at him with cold eyes. Every man's gun hand dangled close to his holster.

Lincoln sighed, and with the calmest of expressions on his face, he opened his hand and let the gun swing down on his trigger finger.

'Then I'll show you I'm a lawman.' He rolled back on his haunches and threw the gun to Zandana's feet. 'Now, I ain't got a gun on you. And I reckon you can listen.'

Zandana snorted as he stood. 'Yeah, you've convinced me: you *ain't* a lawman, and you *are* stupid.'

Zandana gestured to one of his deputies, Raul, who threw him a pair of handcuffs. Zandana caught them one-handed, then directed Lincoln to hold out his hands.

Lincoln shook his head. 'You're not, surely?'

'Not only did you attack me, then pull a gun on me, but you're now resisting arrest. You want to go for some more charges?'

Lincoln winced, then held out his hands for Zandana to grab them and manacle them together.

With a smile now returning to his lips, Zandana tugged Lincoln to his feet, dragged him to the stagecoach, and hurled him inside.

Lincoln resisted the urge to protest, even remaining silent when Zandana ordered him to stay seated and renewed his threats as to what would happen if he gave him any more trouble.

Raul collected Decker and threw him into the stagecoach and on to the seat beside Lincoln, then gathered a six-foot length of chain from another deputy. He doubled the chain over, then attached Lincoln and Decker's handcuffs together.

Again, Lincoln suffered the indignity in silence.

After much tugging to check that the

handcuffs and chains were secure, Raul jumped down and joined the other deputies and Zandana. With much gesticulating in all directions, they debated what to do next.

Through the stagecoach window, Lincoln watched the lawmen, his ear cocked to the side as he strained to hear them, but when he failed to hear enough to understand what they were debating, he slumped back into his seat.

He sensed that Decker was looking at him, but he kept his gaze averted until the strain of having someone staring at him broke him and he turned.

Decker *was* staring at him, with his jaw set in an enquiring smile.

'What you looking at?' Lincoln snarled.

'I don't know. What am I looking at?'

'I'm Marshal Lincoln Hawk,' Lincoln snorted. 'And you're the famous Decker Calhoun, are you?'

'I am.' Decker leaned towards Lincoln and winked. 'But when you're with me, you don't need to claim that you're a lawman.'

'I do,' Lincoln said, feeling his jaw, 'because I am one.'

Decker shrugged, then pulled his chain to drag Lincoln's hands from his face.

'Then that's the stupidest lie I've ever heard.'

'The truth ain't stupid.'

'It is when it gets you a beating.' Decker flexed his back and winced. 'And in my experience, lies get you a beating too.'

Lincoln lowered his voice. 'Zandana has no right to beat one of his prisoners, no matter what his crimes.'

'Tell that to Zandana,' Decker smirked and raised a finger. 'But be warned, if you do, it'll get you another beating.'

Lincoln sighed and stretched back in his seat, searching for a posture that didn't force Decker to lean against him. But they needed a full minute of silent wriggling before they discovered how to play out the chain on the seat in a way that let them sit back and not get in each other's way.

'I can't defend what Zandana did,' Lincoln said, 'but he's dealing with desperate men and that calls for desperate measures. But I'll find a way to make him see reason.'

'You only had one chance to do that.' Decker turned to Lincoln and raised his eyebrows. 'And you've already wasted it.'

Lincoln narrowed his eyes, but on seeing Decker's lively grin, he snorted.

'You mean I should have escaped instead of giving myself up?'

'Yep.'

'I ain't escaping.' Lincoln tugged on the chain binding them together, pulling Decker hard against his shoulder. 'And in case you get any ideas of your own, remember this — I'll ensure you don't escape either.'

Decker pushed away from Lincoln to sit clear of him.

'Because you're a lawman?'

'Because I'm a lawman.'

'Got proof?'

'I'm not on duty.'

Decker blew out his cheeks. 'Either way, Zandana doesn't believe you, and the moment he has no further use for you, he'll kill you, lawman or no lawman.'

'You ain't convincing me of that.' Lincoln folded his arms, dragging Decker's arm to the side. 'But believe this — I ain't siding with you in any plans you're hatching in that devious mind of yours.'

'And I ain't asking you to.' Decker edged to the side to place his mouth beside Lincoln's ear. 'But for the last week my belief that an escape chance will come has fortified me against the beatings.'

'Be quiet. I ain't listening.'

'Then just think about this.' Decker slapped Lincoln's shoulder with the back of his hand, then shuffled away from him. 'A chance will come, and I'll take it. And the only thing that'll keep you alive is taking it with me.'

8

Rocco grabbed his spade, only to hurl it to the ground again, then kick a divot of hard earth at the wall.

With rage contorting his face, he ripped his gun from its holster and aimed down at the ground.

'Don't,' Crane shouted pacing past Wallace to stand in the doorway. 'You can't blast the earth away with bullets.'

'I don't care,' Rocco roared. 'The damn spade ain't doing nothing.'

'Perhaps it ain't, but gunfire will just attract those raiders.' Crane strode to the edge of the hole. 'Put down the gun.'

'But I . . . ' Rocco took long, deep breaths then, muttering to himself, kicked his spade away. He thrust his gun into its holster and stood aside to let Crane wander into the centre of the cleared-away area and tap the ground with his heel.

Only a small lump of dirt broke off and rolled away.

'Any ideas?' Crane said, glancing through the doorway at Wallace and Elwood.

As Wallace and Elwood furrowed their brows, from the adjoining room, chuckling invaded the silence.

Crane swirled round to peer through the doorway and see that Seymour had a hand over his mouth. But his shoulders were shaking with his suppressed mirth.

With Rocco at his heels, Crane stormed through the doorway.

'And what are you finding funny?' he roared.

'I . . . I don't know.' Seymour gulped. 'I guess I thought I was going to die. Then this happens and I just think that . . .'

'And you just think *what*?'

'I guess I'd heard how impressive the Calhoun gang were,' Seymour said, staring at his feet. He lowered his voice to a whisper. 'Suppose they got it wrong.'

As Crane opened and closed his

mouth soundlessly, Rocco barged past him and stormed across the room towards Seymour with his fists raised, but Crane dashed after him and slammed a hand on Rocco's arm.

'Don't threaten our hostages.'

'I ain't threatening no one no more.' Rocco ripped his arm from Crane's grip. 'I'm going to use Seymour's head to hammer the ground until it softens.'

'Rocco,' Crane snapped, 'arguing won't get us our gold. We need to think.'

Rocco snorted and strode another pace, but Seymour fell to his knees and cringed into the corner of the room, his legs wheeling as he pressed himself as far into the corner as he could. Open-mouthed fear replaced his amusement as he raised his hands to ward off Rocco's anticipated blows.

Rocco stared at him, distaste curling his upper lip, then slackened his fists and turned to face Crane.

'All right,' he said, nothing in his flared nostrils and wide eyes suggesting that his anger had abated. 'But stop them taunting us or I will shut someone up, permanently.'

Crane nodded and wandered by Rocco to stare down at the tight ball of arms and legs that was their hostage, Seymour.

'Rocco's right. You were mocking us.'

Seymour peered out from under an arm and finding that Rocco had now backed across the room, he rolled to his knees then feet. With as much dignity as he could muster, he batted the dust from his knees, straightened his jacket, and stood tall.

'I wasn't. I was just . . . '

'You were just, what?'

'He was just scared,' Truman said, spreading his hands. 'Like I guess we all are, and will be until you get the gold and leave us alone.'

'And that's what we want, too,' Crane said, 'but the ground ain't soft enough to dig.'

Truman snorted. 'I can see you men haven't done an honest day's work in your lives. Hard frosts mean hard ground and we aren't expecting the thaw for a while.'

'But the ground shouldn't be that solid inside the house.'

Truman pointed at the open doors. 'Doors have been open all winter, and the frosts have been heavy for the last week.'

'Then what do we do?'

Truman shrugged. 'Wait for the thaw.'

Crane took a deep breath. 'What do we do *today*?'

Truman sauntered across the room and peered through the doorway at Rocco and Wallace's abortive attempt to dig a hole, then pointed at Rocco's spade lying on the ground.

'You need tools a lot stronger than that spade to slice through ground this hard — like a pick-axe.' Truman strode to the hole and joined Crane in stabbing at it with the heel of his boot. 'Or perhaps dynamite.'

With a great roar, Rocco grabbed his

spade and advanced on Truman with it held high above his head. In desperation, Crane swung round and lunged for Rocco's arm. He missed, his grasp closing on air, but Rocco veered to the side to avoid him as he swung the spade. It whistled through the air and, as Truman flinched away, the flailing blade just sliced past his right hip, then gouged into the ground six inches from his heel.

With a wild shriek, Truman danced back to cringe against the wall.

But by the time Rocco had prised the spade from the ground and swung it up again, Wallace and Elwood had both grabbed Rocco's arms and dragged him back to the opposite wall.

'Rocco,' Crane muttered, 'stop this.'

Rocco struggled, but on finding no give in Wallace and Elwood's firm grip, he stood tall and released his hold of the spade.

'I will,' he grunted, then pointed at Truman. 'But he's enjoying this too much.'

'I want this over as much as everyone else,' Truman said, edging along the wall to get even further away from Rocco.

But Rocco rolled his shoulders then hurled Elwood and Wallace from him. He advanced a long pace on Truman, but as Truman backed into a corner, he snorted and planted his feet firmly in the centre of the hole.

'You knew this would happen,' he murmured. 'You knew.'

As Truman lowered his head, Crane stood before Rocco and faced Truman.

'For once Rocco's right,' Crane said. 'You knew we couldn't dig up our gold.'

'I didn't,' Truman whined, looking up and flashing a tentative smile. 'I promised to take you to the gold. And I just thought men who had spent twenty years planning how to get that gold would have had the right tools for the job.'

'We didn't know that you'd reburied it and that the ground would be this hard.'

'You should have . . . ' Truman glanced at the glowering Rocco, then lowered his head.

'Now, think about this,' Crane muttered, 'Rocco is all set to pound somebody's head into the dirt until something softens. And I'll let him do that unless you tell me how we get to our gold.'

Truman glanced at the hole, then back up to Crane.

'I've never faced this problem before.'

Crane slammed his hands on his hips. 'But what would you do if you wanted to dig a hole and the ground was this hard?'

'Yeah,' Rocco muttered, 'like if you wanted to bury somebody.'

As Truman shrugged, Elwood raised a hand.

'If we want to soften the earth,' he said, 'we should build a fire.'

'Good idea,' Crane said, turning from Truman. He glanced at the window to his side then around the small building. 'But we can't. The room ain't big enough for a fire and the smoke has nowhere to go.'

'And if it does go anywhere,' Wallace said, 'it'll just attract those raiders.'

Elwood shrugged. 'Perhaps it will. But I don't reckon we have a choice.'

Crane rubbed his chin, searching for an alternative, but finding none, he nodded. 'A fire it is,' he said. 'And I suppose we'll just have to hope that the fire gets us to our gold before the fire gets those raiders to us.'

9

Lincoln rolled back into the seat to stare through the stagecoach window. To his relief, Decker relented from his efforts to talk him into helping him and looked through the opposite window.

Outside, Zandana sent two deputies into the fog.

In Lincoln's opinion, the fog had lifted somewhat and it must now be easier to pick up Crane's trail as he was on foot. But the deputies returned, shaking their heads.

Zandana sent another two deputies in the opposite direction, but again, they returned within five minutes.

After four expeditions, Zandana called his deputies in for a conference and after much pointing and nodding, Zandana stalked towards the stagecoach.

'Get out,' he roared, standing before the stagecoach door.

'Tell him you're a lawman again,' Decker said, leaning towards Lincoln. 'See how much of a beating you get.'

Lincoln kicked open the door and jumped down from the stagecoach, dragging Decker along behind him.

With a few brisk movements, Zandana unhooked the chain that bound them together. But before Lincoln could enjoy his freedom, Zandana attached chains to both Lincoln and Decker's wrists, then attached those chains to a single metal wristband, which he gave to the bulkiest of his deputies, Raul.

Once he'd checked that his prisoners were secure, Raul clicked the band around a left wrist that was as wide as Decker's calf, then dragged Lincoln and Decker into the stagecoach.

They sat while outside Zandana ordered his deputies to harness the horses to the stagecoach.

Raul shuffled down. But on failing to find a way to sit with both Lincoln and Decker in view, he pushed Decker into the seat opposite him and Lincoln into the centre of his seat while he sat back into the corner.

Lincoln and Decker sat silently while Raul roved his gaze back and forth between them.

Within fifteen minutes, the stagecoach lurched to a start, then headed off down the trail.

'What's your plan?' Decker asked Raul, his voice light and seemingly indifferent.

Raul just glared at him from the corner of his eye, then shuffled back so that his vast form filled the corner of the stagecoach. He pulled a leg up on to the seat and looped a handful of Decker's chain into his left hand, then rested that hand on his knee.

With a long lick of his lips, he spat on the floor, then drew his gun and aimed it at Decker.

'He ain't talkative,' Decker said. 'What you reckon, Lincoln?'

'I reckon he likes the quiet and his own business,' Lincoln said. He played his chain out across the seat, letting him shuffle another foot away from Raul and Decker. 'Just like I do.'

Raul grunted his agreement, but with a sideways glance at each man, Decker smiled.

'You reckon you're closer to the gold?'

'Yeah,' Raul muttered with a sneer. 'But perhaps I'll just beat the exact location out of you.'

'I'd like to see you — '

'Decker,' Lincoln snapped. 'Just be quiet.'

Decker shrugged. 'Just wanted to check that he ain't dumb.'

As Raul firmed his jaw, Decker shuffled back into his seat and pursed his lips, making an obvious show of being quiet.

They trundled along, the gentle swaying of the stagecoach rocking them back and forth. But just like Marvin before, Zandana didn't encourage the new driver to risk any great speed.

But five minutes into their journey,

Raul glanced at Lincoln and chuckled to himself.

'So,' he said, 'you're Lincoln Hawk?'

'That's Marshal Lincoln Hawk,' Lincoln said.

'Been a lawman long?'

'A few years.'

'And when you're busy being a lawman, do you keep all the bad guys like Decker Calhoun here in line?'

'Yep.'

Raul licked his lips. 'And do you normally let the likes of Crane Powell take hostages while you stand by and watch?'

Lincoln glanced through the window at the swirling fog outside, confirming when he saw a tree pass by that the fog was lifting, then set his gaze back on Raul.

'I just did what I thought I had to do to keep innocent bystanders safe. But I misjudged the situation. I didn't expect Crane to take everyone with him.'

'You don't sound like much of a lawman to me. Now me, I never let scum like Decker Calhoun cause trouble in the first place.'

Decker shrugged and edged along his seat.

'Why don't you unchain me?' he said, leaning forward. 'Then you can see if you can stop this piece of scum causing trouble.'

'I ain't doing that.' Raul kicked out, his boot slamming into Decker's knee and tumbling him to the floor. 'And keep away. You ain't sitting that close to me.'

Lincoln winced. 'You got no need to do that.'

'And I reckon I have. But as a lawman you obviously ain't had to deal with the likes of Decker.' Raul grinned, displaying a wide arc of blackened teeth. 'It just makes me reckon you ain't one.'

'I am. And I treat my prisoners right.'

Decker shuffled back on to his seat and slid into the same position as he was before with his hands on his knees and leaning towards Raul.

'I said,' Raul grunted, raising his gun to aim it at Decker's chest, 'stay away from me.'

'Or you'll kill me?' Decker said, smirking.

'You got it.'

'But Zandana won't like that. He wants to keep me alive because he reckons I might help him get the gold. And that means your orders are to do what you need to do to control me, short of killing me.'

Raul sneered, 'Don't risk too much on that.'

Decker shuffled forward on his seat so that he perched on the edge. 'But I am. And that means I'll sit closer to you if I like.' He gulped, then firmed his jaw and belched out a great waft of foul air.

'Get away,' Raul muttered, rocking his leg to the floor and cringing from him.

Lincoln snorted, 'Listen to the man, Decker. You don't need this trouble.'

'And,' Decker said, 'I just reckon you

need to see what kind of man you're supporting.'

Decker edged towards Raul another six inches.

Raul pulled on his chain, aiming to tug Decker to the floor, but with surprising strength, Decker bunched his fists and resisted, even pulling Raul a few inches from his seat. Raul relented from his tugging, and, with a smirk, Decker shuffled along his seat to sit perched in the corner of the stagecoach, his face just two feet from Raul's gun.

'Now, that's right comfortable,' he murmured. 'But being as you don't seem to mind, I might just get closer and closer and closer to you.'

Decker rolled from his seat and knelt before Raul.

'Get away,' Raul grunted, 'or you'll be writhing on the floor with a bullet in your guts.'

Decker smiled and shuffled even closer, his nose now just a foot from Raul's gun.

Raul breathed deeply, then with a

wild roar, backhanded his gun at Decker's face. Decker jerked his head back from the blow, but it still clubbed into his temple, knocking him against the side of the stagecoach for him to rebound and slump to the floor between the seats.

'You didn't need to do that,' Lincoln murmured. 'The old-timer was just amusing himself.'

Raul swirled his gun to the side to train it on Lincoln.

'Be quiet or you'll be next.'

'I won't.' Lincoln shook his head, then looked Raul up and down, sneering. 'And I reckon I'll make some reports when this is over and then, you'll be back in jail with Decker.'

'Reports! You know nothing about being a lawman.'

From the floor Decker gurgled a pained screech, and Lincoln glanced down to see a bubble of blood escape his lips.

Lincoln winced. 'You've really hurt him.'

Lincoln moved to slip from his seat, but Raul firmed his gun hand.

'Old-timer's just faking it. Stay where you are.'

But Lincoln snorted and slipped from the seat to kneel beside Decker. He placed his hands on either side of Decker's head and shook him, but it was only to receive a thicker stream of blood from his lips.

'I ain't no doctor,' Lincoln said, 'but this man is in trouble. Help him.'

'Quit worrying,' Raul said. He kicked Decker's shoulder. 'Old fool is just getting himself some sleep.'

Lincoln felt Decker's clammy brow, then glared up at Raul. 'He ain't.'

Raul feigned a yawn. 'I ain't wasting my time. Now, get on the seat before you get the same.'

'For the last time,' Lincoln snapped, 'help him!'

'For the last time!' Raul raised a fist, pulling the chain between him and Lincoln taut. 'What kind of talk is that?'

'The kind you'll listen to if you don't

125

want to go against Zandana's orders and kill Decker.'

Raul snorted, but then with a sharp nod, directed Lincoln to back from Decker and sit. He rolled to the floor. On one knee, he grabbed Decker's comatose body and dragged him up on to the seat beside him.

Decker just lolled back on his seat, his mouth open and dribbling blood, his eyes open and rolling.

'There, I've helped him. Now quit whining, or I'll do this.' Raul grinned and kicked Decker's slack legs from under him, bundling him to the floor again.

His unexpected action pulled Decker's chain taut and dragged Lincoln to the floor, too, tumbling him over Decker.

Lincoln lay a moment, anger burning his guts. But as Raul laughed and again kicked Decker's sprawled legs, he rolled back and slammed his fist backhanded at Raul's chest.

Trapped in the corner of the stagecoach, Raul couldn't avoid the blow, but he shrugged it off, then swung his gun round to aim it at Lincoln's head. But with his other hand, Lincoln lunged and grabbed the gun, pushing it high.

Raul flexed his arm, his jaw muscles bunching as he tried to pull the gun down, but finding that Lincoln's grip was firm, he relented, and with his free hand grabbed the chain binding him to Decker. He dragged a length free then looped it and whipped the end at Lincoln's head.

Lincoln saw the blow coming and flinched from it, but it still flailed around his neck, the links grinding into his flesh.

Raul grinned and ripped back the chain ready for a second stronger blow, but when it came, Lincoln released his grip of Raul's gun hand and at the same time ducked. From so close, Raul's wild blow whipped in a short arc over Lincoln's head and Raul clipped his own elbow.

Raul screeched. His arm flailed as the

blow deadened his hand muscles, letting the gun fly from his slack fingers. The gun tumbled end over end before it slammed into the seat opposite.

Both Lincoln and Raul glanced at the gun. Then they both hurled themselves at it.

Lincoln stumbled, his attachment to Decker impeding him, but Raul, with his longer reach, vaulted into the other seat and grabbed the gun with his left hand. He spun round in the seat to stare down at Lincoln, who, with no choice, backed into the opposite seat, raising his hands.

With an angry grunt, Raul grabbed a firm grip of the chain and dragged the prone Decker along the floor until he bumped into the side of the seat.

Raul tugged again, but on failing to drag Decker from the floor, he relented and backed into the corner. But Decker's chain had wrapped itself tightly around his right leg and, to free himself, he pulled Decker to a sitting position, leaning him back against the door.

'Now, Lincoln,' he said, shrugging his arm to play out the chain on the seat beside him, 'you just did a whole mess of things wrong. As you're a lawman, you want to list 'em?'

Lincoln shook his head. 'I only tried to stop you hurting Decker.'

'Sounds enough to me.' Raul firmed his gun hand.

'You won't kill me,' Lincoln said, jutting his chin. 'Those ain't your orders.'

Raul's right eye twitched. Then he glanced down at the prone Decker and smiled.

'But that don't stop me getting myself a quiet journey. Decker's gone all quiet, and so can you.' He swung the gun round in his grip and rolled from his seat, the stock held out and ready to pistol-whip Lincoln. 'Just don't struggle and you won't feel a thing.'

'Stop,' Lincoln murmured, jerking his head back from the advancing Raul.

Raul shrugged and raised the stock as he paced over Decker. Then he shrieked.

For a moment Lincoln couldn't see why. Then he saw that Decker had thrust his head up and had clamped an arc of yellowing teeth into Raul's right calf.

Acting on impulse and with no time to ponder how Decker was now conscious, Lincoln leapt to his feet and grabbed Raul's gun arm.

With Decker digging his teeth into Raul's leg, and with Lincoln gripping his arm and holding the gun high, they pushed Raul back against the door.

The door creaked, protesting the extra weight. Then it flew open.

Below, the dregs of fog wreathing the hard ground whipped by as, on the edge of the open door, all three men tottered. Then Decker grabbed a firm grip of Raul's legs and hurled himself through the door.

For the briefest of moments Lincoln

dug his heels in, but the trailing chains yanked him through the door after them and tumbled him from the stagecoach.

10

With a few barked commands, Crane ordered his men to drag the furniture into the other room and prepare it for a fire.

Rocco didn't need any encouragement to smash everything he could lay his hands on into firewood against the wall.

Truman bleated when Rocco crashed an ornate chair to the ground, but a firm glare from Crane silenced him.

Within minutes, Rocco had converted the furniture to a heap of firewood, the effort subduing his seething anger to a low murmuring and a deeply furrowed brow.

Elwood piled the heap of wood over their attempt to dig a hole, then lit a fire. With the only kindling being some cloth and paper, which he'd gathered from a now-demolished drawer, it took him long minutes to coax a flame.

But with much blowing and shuffling

on hands and knees around the pile of wood, he produced smoke, then flames. Once he'd encouraged those first fragile flames into life, the slight breeze blowing through the doorway to the window moved the air with sufficient strength to whip the flames into a roaring blaze.

Within minutes, the fire grew to consume the remnants of the furniture. Luckily, the breeze was also strong enough to direct the smoke through the window and keep the air in the adjoining room breathable.

And the extra warmth enlivened Crane's sagging spirits and even encouraged Rocco to hold out his hands and warm them.

Crane ordered Wallace to guard the doorway and watch for the raiders approaching, then invited Elwood and the hostages to stand around the fire and warm themselves.

But he grabbed Truman's arm and held him back.

'How long before this fire works?' he asked.

'No idea,' Truman said. 'Ask Elwood. This was his idea.'

'But I'm asking you what you think will happen.'

'And why would . . . So, you still think I'm playing a trick on you.' Truman sighed and pointed around the room that now lacked furniture. 'But I'm not. And you'd better hope this works. After that, you have nothing left to burn.'

Rocco snorted and wandered from the fire to loom over Truman.

'No,' he muttered, stabbing a finger at Truman's chest that knocked him back a pace. 'You'd better hope this works.'

'Rocco,' Crane said, 'give everyone a rest and stop threatening our hostages every chance you get.'

Rocco flared his eyes, but with encouragement from Elwood, he wandered back into the other room and watched the smoke billow out of the window. But he cradled his gun in the crook of his elbow and tapped his foot on the ground with an insistent rhythm.

'Obliged to you for speaking up for me,' Truman said. 'Again. But I'd be happier if you'd just trust me. I want this to end as much as you do.'

'Yeah, but Rocco was right. You'd better hope this works.'

Truman sighed and shook his head. 'Crane, I hear your threats. But I've heard of the Calhoun gang. However badly you want that gold, you won't kill us.'

'Decker always said you should avoid doing that.' Crane blew out his cheeks and turned on the spot to look at the fire, then sighed and turned back to face Truman. 'But don't get too confident. He ain't in charge now.'

'But I've been watching you and I reckon you're still trying to act with some decency.'

'I guess I am.' Crane gathered Truman round to look at Rocco. 'But believe this — if we don't reach our gold soon, I won't be able to stop Rocco taking out his frustration on someone. His anger has festered for twenty years. And I reckon you'll be the first one on the receiving end.'

'Then you'll have to stop him.'

'Why should I bother? I don't exactly trust you.'

Truman closed his eyes a moment. 'Have no doubt — the gold is in this summer house.'

'So you keep saying.' Crane sighed and glanced at Truman from the corner of his eye, considering the sharpness of his tailored suit, the clean boots, the absence of patches adorning his clothing. 'And you're still claiming that you never touched our gold?'

'I did nothing,' Truman murmured. 'I was tempted I'll admit that, but I decided that fate and maybe God was testing me. So, I reburied the gold and doubled my efforts to survive without it. And I did. I never used that gold.'

Crane shook his head. 'I don't believe you. Nobody could have resisted the temptation.'

'But I did. I reckoned that the gold

was my lifetime's temptation. Whenever conditions were harsh, I would again have to resist the lure of the easy option. And I always did and always sought my own solutions.' Truman puffed his chest and tucked his thumbs into his waistcoat pockets. 'That gold made me the successful man I am today. Not through using it, but through my determination to avoid using it.'

'Well, I ain't got that much determination.'

'But perhaps you should search for it in yourself. You've spent twenty years in jail. But there's so much more you can do with the rest of your life, and trying to get this gold will just get you killed.'

'Or get me our gold. And after twenty years, I've earned it.'

'You've earned nothing. Do something else instead where the reward comes from your honest efforts. Perhaps if you resist, you can be as successful as I am.' Truman rubbed his chin, then raised a finger. 'Why not — ?'

'Enough,' Crane snapped. 'I'm getting our gold.'

Truman raised his hands, then paced from Crane to join the rest of the hostages in staring at the fire and warming himself.

Crane stared at Truman's back, then shrugged and joined him. With his hands held out, he stared deep into the flames, trying to let the heat warm more than just his body.

But he couldn't shake his growing fear that no matter what he did, he just wasn't getting any closer to their gold.

Those four feet of earth might as well be a hundred miles.

Minute by minute the fire built until it reached its most intense point, the heat blistering within the confines of the building and baking Crane's skin, the light casting flickering red shadows on the walls.

'When will this work?' Crane asked Elwood.

'It should have done already,' Elwood said. 'Once the fire has died down, we'll drag it to the side, dig down as far as we can, then pile the fire back in the new hole for the heat to penetrate deeper.'

'And that'll work?' Rocco grunted.

Elwood kneaded his forehead. 'Perhaps we ain't got enough wood, but we still ought to be — '

'You never said we didn't have enough wood.'

'I don't know,' Elwood said, shrugging. 'Perhaps we have or perhaps we ain't.'

Rocco snorted and grabbed an unburnt chair leg from the side of the fire.

'I've had enough of this,' he muttered, swiping the leg through the flames. 'I'm going to — !'

'Rocco,' Crane shouted. 'Patience!'

'I lost that back in the trading post. And I reckon we got too many hostages.' Rocco swirled round and patted the leg into his other palm as he glared at each of their hostages in turn. 'We don't need them all.'

'Rocco, we don't kill. Remember

Decker's orders.'

'And that was twenty years ago, and Decker ain't around to boss us no more.'

'Listen to Crane,' Truman said, pacing to Crane's side. 'Don't hurt anyone.'

'Oh?' Rocco muttered, his eyes gleaming red in the light from the fire. 'I wasn't aiming to hurt just *anyone*.'

Truman stood tall and glanced at the circle of people standing around the fire, then centred his gaze on Rocco.

'I believe Crane, Elwood and Wallace could be more than just failed thieves. But you're different. You've been spoiling for a fight ever since you walked into the trading post.'

Rocco chuckled. 'You noticed.'

Truman raised his fists, then danced on the spot, his feet whirring as he feigned blows at an imaginary opponent.

'I did. And I reckon now is the time you'll get one.'

With his mouth falling open, Rocco

looked Truman up and down, appraising his fists, and the short blows he was ripping right and left.

'You can't mean you?' he murmured.

'I fought long and hard to get what I have today. I can knock sense into the likes of you.'

'You don't know how to fight.' Rocco hurled the chair leg into the heart of the fire.

'I know the rules of gentlemanly conduct, which are sometimes required to resolve conflict. And I will observe those rules. Other than that, you will get the thrashing you deserve.'

Rocco glanced at Crane, who was staring at Truman with the same wide-eyed bemusement that everyone else in the room was.

'I guess I can't stop this,' Crane murmured. He nodded, but held out a hand for Rocco's gunbelt.

With his grin threatening to consume his face, Rocco unhooked the belt and threw it to Crane.

'Come on, then,' Rocco said. He

cracked his knuckles, then beckoned Truman to approach. 'Let's see what the rules of gentlemanly conduct will get you.'

Truman lowered his fists, then shrugged his jacket from his shoulders. But, as he was extricating himself from the sleeves, Rocco stormed two long paces and hurled a blow at his chin. Caught in his jacket, Truman couldn't avoid the blow, and by the time he'd ripped his arms free, Rocco had already bundled him to the ground with a flurry of blows.

Rocco stood over him, grinning.

'I wasn't ready,' Truman murmured, fingering his chin.

'And I learnt the rules of gentlemanly conduct in Barton jail. And there, nobody stood around waiting for a fight to start.'

Rocco grabbed Truman's arm and dragged him to his feet. He stood him tall then pummelled him against the wall, knocking his hat to the ground, but Truman rebounded and hurled a flailing round-armed punch at Rocco's head.

Rocco ducked the blow and launched himself at Truman, flattening him to the wall. He grabbed a tuft of hair on the top of his head and slammed his head against the wall, then slammed it again and danced back.

Truman staggered away from the wall, his eyes rolling, but Rocco grabbed his right arm in both hands and flung him in a short arc.

Truman wheeled from Rocco's grip, heading straight for the fire, but in a frantic leap, he tumbled over it. He landed heavily and rolled, crashing into the wall.

On his side he lay a moment, but Rocco leapt over the fire and with a great roar, slammed both hands down on his back. He pulled him from the ground, suspending his entire body momentarily in the air before he crashed him down on his feet.

Truman tottered, but Rocco grabbed his shoulders, keeping him from falling.

When he was sure Truman wouldn't fall, he locked both hands together, then swung his two great fists into Truman's cheek, sending him looping in a circle before he crashed into the wall, then slid to the ground.

Truman thrust both hands flat to the ground and flexed his shoulders, trying to rise, but then with a heavy sigh, relented and plummeted back to the ground.

With this final blow, Rocco stood tall and batted his hands.

'Now, that felt good,' he said. 'Anyone else want sense knocked into them?'

He glanced at Seymour and Marvin, but neither of them met his eye.

With jerking movements, Truman straightened and rolled on to his back.

'You haven't finished me,' he said. 'I've fought and overcome bigger obstacles than the likes of you.'

Rocco grinned and strode towards Truman, but Crane shook his head and paced round to stand before him with a hand raised.

'That's enough,' he said. He seized Rocco's arm and pulled him away from Truman. 'You got no reason to carry this on.'

'Perhaps he hasn't,' Truman murmured from the ground, 'but I do.'

Shaking his head, Crane turned. 'But why?'

'Because I have to show you that you aren't like Rocco. He's a vicious bully, but *you* don't have to threaten us. Just end this and walk away from that — '

'I can't do that,' Crane roared, pointing a firm finger at Truman.

'Then I can't walk away from this fight.'

'You can't even walk right now. Just stay down.'

Truman snorted. He pushed his hands to the ground and levered himself to a sitting position, then to his knees. Finally, he stood, his clothes now dirt-streaked, his face puffy and reddened. He raised his fists, although the arms shook.

'Rocco,' he muttered, 'I'm ready to end this.'

Rocco chuckled and ripped back a fist. 'If you insist.'

By the door, Wallace coughed.

'Stop that,' he shouted, beckoning Crane and Rocco to join him with a sharp wave of his arm.

Rocco glared at Truman a moment longer, then lowered his fist.

'What's wrong?' Crane asked, pacing from the fire.

Wallace stood to the side of the door until Crane joined him, then pointed through the doors.

'The fog is lifting.'

Crane glanced over Wallace's shoulder at the terrain, noting that he could now see the outline of the ridge against the sky.

'Ain't worried about that.'

'Yeah, but the trouble is — I can see a whole lot further now. And I can see what's coming.'

Wallace pointed at a line of shapes wading through the last sparse tendrils of fog.

Even as Crane looked, the shapes

coalesced into the forms of the riders heading down the side of the ridge towards them.

Crane gulped. 'And those raiders are coming.'

11

With their chains clumping them together, Lincoln, Decker and Raul hurtled from the stagecoach. In a tangled sprawl, they hit the ground and rolled from the trail to flop to a scraping halt beside a ditch.

Zandana and the other deputies were ahead of the lead horses, and as Lincoln shook his head to regain his senses, the driver cried out that he'd seen them fall. But the stagecoach was travelling fast enough to disappear into the fog within moments.

Lincoln staggered to his knees, numbness from his bruised body slowing his actions, only to find that Decker had looped a length of chain around Raul's neck and was staring at him. But in his grip, Raul lay slack-mouthed and possibly unconscious.

Lincoln grabbed Decker in a neck-hold and prised him away from Raul, but Decker rolled with Lincoln's pull and the three men fell into the ditch in a heap.

From down the trail, cries ripped through the air as Zandana and the other lawmen doubled back to recapture them.

Lincoln edged up ready to leap to his feet and alert them, but Decker grabbed his arm, halting him.

'Don't,' he said, pulling Lincoln round to face him. 'This is our chance.'

'I told you,' Lincoln muttered, 'no matter what the provocation from these men, I'm not helping you escape.'

Hoofs thundered as Zandana and his deputies closed on them.

'Just give me time to tell you my story.' Decker released his hold of Raul, letting him slump at his feet. He darted his gaze over Lincoln's shoulder, then fixed him with his earnest gaze. 'If you alert Zandana, you'll die. If you don't,

149

and we escape, you can still alert him later.'

Lincoln glanced over his shoulder to see a rider emerge from the fog.

In a sudden decision, Lincoln dropped into the ditch. A moment later Decker dropped to lie beside him and the three men lay prone.

To his side, Lincoln heard the deputy approach, then clatter by. Then more riders clumped past, stopping around fifteen yards to his right.

'Spread out,' Zandana roared. 'They're close.'

Horses thundered in all directions, one deputy even vaulting over their ditch.

'They have to find us,' Lincoln whispered. He glanced up, but saw nothing but the deserted trail fading into the fog on either side of them.

'I've spent every moment since I left jail planning how to escape,' Decker whispered, pulling Lincoln down to lie beside him. 'And ever since this fog came down, I've reckoned it's my best chance. Zandana expects me to run and if I did, he'd pick up my trail no matter where I went.'

'And going nowhere leaves no trail.' Lincoln snorted. 'That ain't much to put your faith in.'

'It's all I have.'

Lincoln and Decker burrowed down on either side of the prone Raul, searching for that extra inch of hiding space in the shallow ditch.

Every second, Lincoln expected Zandana to take his decision away from him and find them, but aside from the occasional irritated holler from Zandana's deputies, they showed no sign of closing on them.

Within ten minutes, the deputies returned to a spot some thirty yards down the trail — far enough away that Lincoln couldn't see them, but close enough that he could hear Zandana's barked orders.

To Lincoln's surprise, Zandana ordered his deputies to give up the search and head down the trail again after Crane.

Within a minute, hoofbeats clumped

away and the stagecoach resumed its journey.

Lincoln glanced up and confirmed that they were, in fact, alone.

'Surprised?' Decker asked, joining Lincoln in peering down the trail.

'Yep.'

'I ain't. Zandana reckons he knows where I'll go.'

'After the gold?'

'Yeah.' Decker opened his mouth wide and prodded the inside of his cheek, then glanced at his bloodied finger. 'Wish I hadn't bit myself so hard to get some blood.'

'I should have realized you weren't hurt. But I now have a decision to make.' Lincoln shuffled away from Decker as far as his chain would allow. 'So, tell me a story that'll convince me I was right not to alert Zandana.'

'I will.' Decker shuffled round to face Lincoln and rested a foot on Raul's side. 'But tell me this first — why did Zandana beat you?'

'He reckoned I was trouble.' Lincoln

shuffled down to gain a more comfortable sitting position on the side of the ditch. 'But I'll just have to convince him that I'm a lawman later.'

'But you won't get the chance. A lawman will be the first to die when Zandana finds the gold.' Decker laughed without humour. 'So, if I were you, I'd come up with a better story.'

'What you mean?'

'I mean you figured out that Zandana took me from Barton jail to help him locate the gold.' Decker leaned forward and snorted. 'But you didn't figure out that when he finds the gold, he won't send me back to jail.'

'You mean you did a deal with Zandana and he'll let you go?'

'Nope. He'll kill me. And that ain't the worst of it.' Decker glanced down the trail, a long sigh escaping his lips. 'He'll keep the gold, too.'

'Zandana wouldn't do that,' Lincoln murmured.

'Perhaps he's not the only one who's spent the last twenty years thinking about the gold that got away.'

'He's still a lawman.'

'Even lawmen think, and you've seen how ruthless he is. Raul almost killed you back in the stagecoach.'

'But he didn't. He just tried to control me.'

Decker glanced down at Raul and tapped him with his foot, receiving a subdued moan.

'It looked like he was just beating you to me.'

'He let me know how determined he was, but fell short of killing me.'

'Wrong. He kept you alive because that was Zandana's orders.'

Lincoln glanced at Raul, then at Decker. But Decker was looking at him with his eyebrows raised and the directness of his wide-eyed gaze bored into Lincoln's mind demanding that he believed every word he'd just uttered.

Lincoln rolled to his knees and knelt on the edge of the ditch.

'It can't be,' he murmured, rubbing his chin as he fought down the dread thought that Decker could be right. Then he smiled. 'And it ain't. If you're right, Zandana would have killed me the moment I walked into his camp and claimed I was a lawman.'

'And he nearly did. But I saw the look in your eyes when Zandana asked you whether you knew where the gold was. You knew, but you didn't tell him because you already feared he might have another plan in mind. And if I saw that look, so did Zandana. And that was the only thing that kept you alive.'

Lincoln shuffled round to look away from Decker.

'Whatever you say,' he said, the shock that he was only just choking back coarsening his voice, 'I ain't letting you escape.'

'And what about the gold? Are you letting Zandana escape with that? Because he won't leave any witnesses to what he's planning to do. And that includes, you, me, Crane.' Decker sighed. 'And even those hostages.'

Lincoln swirled round to face Decker.

'I can't believe that.'

Decker shrugged. 'So, if you won't listen, what are we doing?'

'There is no *we*. I'm getting to the gold and helping my fellow lawmen. And then I'll . . . then I'll . . . ' Lincoln threw his bound hands above his head, pulling Decker forward. 'And then I'll figure out the rest later.'

Decker jutted his chin and stamped his foot.

'Then I'm going nowhere.'

Lincoln tugged on his chain, but Decker firmed his back and glared at a spot just above Lincoln's right shoulder.

Lincoln half-heartedly tugged the chain again, then slipped into the ditch. He rummaged through Raul's pockets, but on failing to find a key to either their chains or their handcuffs, he looped an arm under Raul's armpit and pulled him to his feet.

Decker planted his feet firmly in the ditch and remained seated. Lincoln tugged but Decker had flexed his bony form and he failed to move him an inch.

Without Raul to deal with, Lincoln could have slung Decker over his shoulder and carried him as far as he liked. But with the bulky Raul on one arm, he wasn't going anywhere that Decker didn't want to go.

Lincoln swung round and stared down at him.

'Come on, Decker. I did what I promised. I listened to your story. Now I'm leaving.'

'And I ain't.' Decker grinned and shuffled down into the earth. 'And you can't drag me and Raul.'

Lincoln looked to the fog-shrouded sky, then down to Decker.

'All right,' he murmured. 'What will it take for you to help?'

'A promise to let me go.'

'Try again.'

Decker tipped back his hat to scratch his forehead, then nodded.

'Best I can offer is — promise me you'll find out whether my story is true before you rejoin Zandana, and if it is, you'll help me to get away.'

Lincoln closed his eyes a moment, then nodded.

'I suppose I can agree to that.' Lincoln watched Decker grin. 'But I will come for you after I've sorted out everything else.'

'I know. I only want a chance to escape. And I'll back myself to hide from you.'

As Lincoln snorted, Decker widened his grin and jumped to his feet. He grabbed Raul's other arm and, with an arm apiece draped over their shoulders, they dragged him from the ditch, his feet trailing behind him.

In keeping with his promise to Decker, Lincoln let them walk about thirty yards off the trail, keeping it in view, but far enough away that if Zandana doubled back they had enough time to hide.

But this precaution had a lessening effect as the afternoon sun burned away the fog with increasing speed.

Even so, with Raul's bulky form weighing them down, they made painfully slow progress.

At a corner to the trail where the route swung east towards Sweetwater, the stagecoach emerged from the fog ahead. It was stationary and nobody was beside it, even the horses were standing quietly, but they slowed then approached it in a cautious arc.

A slow circuit confirmed that Zandana had abandoned it and they found his tracks heading off the trail and uphill towards the mist-shrouded ridge to their side.

With both he and Decker breathing heavily, Lincoln ordered a rest.

'You'd have thought Zandana would have caught up with Crane by now,' Lincoln said, rubbing his strained arms. 'Crane is walking and he's guarding his hostages.'

'I ain't sure Zandana's following Crane. He followed him earlier in the week. And he knows the gold is on the other side of the ridge.' Decker pointed uphill. 'But he doesn't know exactly where.'

'And where *exactly* did you bury it?' Lincoln said.

'I reckon you already know that.' Decker rolled to his feet and stood, creaking his strained back into a straight position. 'But you'd better find a way to free us from Raul, or we'll never drag him up and over that ridge.'

Lincoln tugged at the chains, finding no suggestion of give, then considered Raul's bulky form.

'You got any ideas?'

'I have.' Decker glanced at the stagecoach.

Lincoln followed the direction of Decker's stare. He nodded as he considered how he might safely use the wheels to roll over the chains and break through them, but no matter what set of actions he devised, his plans were all dangerous.

He turned back to Decker.

But it was only to find that Decker had a gun in his hand and had aimed it at his chest.

Lincoln rubbed his eyes, chiding himself for forgetting to search for Raul's gun when he'd rolled into the ditch.

'I was just beginning to believe you never meant anyone any harm,' Lincoln said, raising his hands to waist level. 'But turning a gun on a lawman ain't helping that belief.'

'And I won't shoot you. I'll just free me from Raul. Then it's up to you what you want to do.'

Decker edged back to gain himself the maximum distance from Lincoln, then raised his chain and dangled it before the gun. At the first attempt he shot through the chain connecting him to Raul, then rolled free.

'Don't run,' Lincoln said.

Decker shrugged and backed a pace from Lincoln. He blasted through the chain connecting his handcuffs, then spread both his arms, flexing the muscles and smiling at the relief.

But then gunfire echoed nearby.

Decker dropped to his knees, then

shuffled behind the nearest boulder while Lincoln rolled over the prone Raul and peered up the ridge.

The high sun was burning away the last of the fog and he could now see the outline of the angular ridge against the sky.

The gunfire blasted again, and this time, Lincoln reckoned it came from the other side of the ridge. So he sat, as Decker rolled out from behind the boulder.

Decker gestured for Lincoln to remove Raul's gunbelt then peered in all directions as he wrapped the belt around his waist.

'If you free me from Raul,' Lincoln said, 'I'll speak up for you.'

'I ain't doing that.' Decker stood and backed away from Lincoln to peer at the ridge. 'And if you have any sense, you'll keep your head down here. If not, I wish you luck.'

'You won't get that gold.'

Decker rubbed his chin, a mischievous smile invading his features.

'You just don't understand me. I know of something a whole lot better than gold — freedom.'

'You're right there, but once I'm free and have released those hostages, I will come for you.'

Decker pointed towards the direction of the shooting.

'Well, if it helps, the gold, Crane, Zandana and all that shooting is that way.' Decker pointed over his shoulder. 'And I'm heading that way.'

Decker turned and paced away. At a steady pace, he wandered by the stagecoach and headed down the trail towards Sweetwater.

'I know you're trying to confuse me as to where you're heading,' Lincoln shouted after him. 'But it won't work. I'll be right behind you once I've sorted out the rest.'

Decker walked for another five paces, then stopped and turned.

'But why?' he said, wandering back towards Lincoln with his hands upturned. 'I stole a whole mess of gold twenty years ago. I didn't hurt anyone, and soon several former lawmen will have stolen the gold for themselves. Why punish me any further?'

'If you have to ask, I can't answer.'

Decker sighed and stomped to a halt. 'You won't take my advice to not rejoin Zandana, will you?'

'Nope. I have my duty and I have to help free those hostages.' Lincoln looped an arm under Raul's back and dragged him to his feet. 'And I'll do that, whatever the cost.'

'Joining Zandana won't free anyone.' Decker kicked at the earth and sighed. 'But you seem like you're a man who always keeps his word.'

With Raul dangling from his grasp, Lincoln shuffled round in a circle to face Decker.

'I am.'

'Then if you give me your word that you won't go after me, I'll shoot through your chains and give you a better chance to free those hostages.' Decker raised his eyebrows. 'But please do it without seeking Zandana's help.'

'No deal. You're asking me to let a jailbird go free, and I can't do that.'

Decker whistled under his breath. 'Guess you do keep your word. You could have let me free you, then gone back on your promise.'

'I could have. But I didn't.'

'Obliged.' Decker sighed. 'Then take this advice — you gained Crane's confidence. Use that. It's your only advantage.'

'Obliged.' Lincoln flashed a smile. 'See you later, Decker.'

Decker returned the smile, then turned and took two steady paces. He wavered then swung back and pulled his gun. With one eye closed, he sighted the chain connecting Lincoln to Raul and shot through it.

Lincoln glanced at the broken chain dangling from his arm, then lowered Raul to the ground. He flexed his arms, enjoying feeling the lack of Raul's weight dragging on them, then spread his hands as wide as he could above his head.

Decker shot through his handcuff chain.

'Why?' Lincoln asked, rolling his wrists and shrugging the tautness from his arms.

Decker licked his lips. 'If you have to ask, I can't answer.'

Decker tipped his hat and walked backwards from Lincoln. He'd walked ten paces when Lincoln raised a hand.

'All right, Decker,' he said. 'You've convinced me you're a decent man. Perhaps we can . . . '

Lincoln sighed and lowered his head a moment, then looked up, but try as he might he couldn't complete his offer.

Decker walked another three paces before he stopped and raised his eyebrows.

'You offering a deal?' he asked.

Lincoln glanced over his shoulder at the ridge, then at Decker. He took a deep breath.

'I guess I am. It's like this . . . '

12

On either side of the door Elwood and Wallace kept guard, firing sporadically whenever the raiders ventured a shot at them.

While Rocco guarded one of the back windows, Crane ordered Marvin to drag the embers of the fire back, which he managed while still keeping the fire alight. With Truman sitting in the corner nursing his bruises, Crane ordered Seymour to dig.

As Crane had hoped, the fire had turned the top layer of soil to thick mud, and further down the ground was soft enough to dig, but not quickly.

After a few minutes, Marvin relieved the rapidly tiring Seymour, but the digging didn't proceed much faster. Each spadeful was hard-won and he was exhausted by the time he'd dug out a foot of earth.

With his men guarding the door well enough to keep the men outside from getting closer than a tangle of boulders one hundred yards up the ridge, Crane grabbed a spade and joined Marvin in hammering the ground.

After only scraping away another few inches, he relented and swapped places at the window with Rocco.

For his part Rocco attacked the hole with vigour. In the central depression, he gouged a deep furrow, while Marvin and Seymour stood on the outside of the hole, wiping sweat from their brows and shaking their heads at the slow progress.

Truman crawled to the edge of the hole, and from the hopeful smile on his lips, Crane consoled himself with the belief that he appeared to be expecting the casket to appear at any moment.

With a long sigh, Crane hunkered down beside Truman and peered into the hole, shaking his head.

'We're two feet down,' he said,

keeping his voice level. 'The casket must be close.'

'It *is* there,' Truman said, wiping his brow.

'And it'd better be. I got a feeling that after this much digging, Rocco won't be in the mood for failure.'

'Too right,' Rocco muttered, then slammed his spade down again.

'Trust me,' Truman said.

'I hope I can.' Crane grabbed Truman's bruised chin and rocked his head from side to side, considering the numerous bruises emerging from the skin. 'But it worries me that you seem to have got yourself a death wish.'

Truman shrugged from Crane's grip and crawled back from the hole to lean on the wall.

'I was just demonstrating to you what's at stake here.'

Crane sauntered to Truman's side and stood over him, shaking his head.

'You only proved that you can't fight as well as Rocco can.'

'I knew that already, but once you've

thought some more, you'll see that I'm right.' Truman pointed at Rocco who was now cursing as his progress slowed. 'You're not like that brute. You don't need gold to sort out your life.'

Crane waved a dismissive hand at Truman, then strode to the side of the hole.

In only five minutes Rocco had hammered out another foot of earth, but now his efforts were waning and the casket still hadn't emerged from the dirt.

Rocco stood aside to let Crane jump into the hole and kick at the solid earth beneath his feet. He dropped to his knees and fingered the earth. The ground wasn't as cold as he expected, the thick frost that had hardened the surface not penetrating this deep.

'You reckon the fire will help?' he asked.

Rocco shrugged. 'Ain't sure. I reckon we're through the frost, but the ground is just getting harder. But I guess it won't hurt to try.'

Crane nodded and levered himself from the hole, then ordered Marvin to pile the remnants of the fire back into the hole to soften more earth.

But as Marvin grabbed the spare spade, a prolonged burst of gunfire sounded outside.

Rocco leapt from the hole and dashed to the back window as Crane joined Wallace at the side of the doorway.

But unlike the cannoning series of blasts that had peppered the walls earlier, none of this gunfire landed near the summer house.

Crane glanced outside. He put a hand to his brow, shielding his eyes from the lowering sun, and confirmed that the raiders hadn't left the tangle of rocks at the base of the ridge. But whenever one of them lifted to fire, he aimed away from the house and up the ridge.

With Wallace covering him, Crane edged out from the house a pace and peered at the ridge, searching along the mess of boulders and scree for the location of the shooter. But pockets of fog still clung to the ground, impeding his vision and he saw no movement.

'Suppose we should have realized that we wouldn't be the only ones after our gold,' he murmured, backing into the house.

'Yeah,' Wallace said, 'but how many groups are out there?'

'Who cares? While they're arguing amongst themselves, we can run.'

Another volley of gunshots blasted, this time sounding as if the firing came from the side of the house. Then Rocco turned from the back window.

'Hey, Crane,' he shouted, 'come see this.'

Crane peered outside another moment, then dashed from the doorway to the window.

Through the window he saw that a hundred yards away a man was sprinting towards the summer house.

Crane narrowed his eyes and to his surprise realized the man was Lincoln.

'Wallace,' he shouted, 'I need covering fire. Lincoln's rejoining us.'

Wallace and Elwood leapt into the doorway and took turns to blast at the raiders, peppering the rocks behind which they were hiding and forcing them to dive for cover whenever they bobbed up.

Outside, Lincoln dashed the last few yards to the house, then pressed himself flat against the wall. Rocco called for him to come in, and with a helping hand, dragged him on to the window ledge.

'Can't say I ever expected to see you again,' Crane said as Lincoln rolled into the building, then batted the dust from his clothing.

Lincoln smiled. 'I can think of fifty thousand reasons why you would. Even if you abandoned me.'

Crane shrugged. 'We took our chances.'

'Yeah.' Lincoln glanced at the fire in the hole, then skirted round it. At the front door, he considered the raiders' position, nodded, then turned to Crane.

'You got the gold yet?'

'It's buried.' Crane pointed at the fire. 'Beneath that damn fire.'

Lincoln narrowed his eyes, but then kicked at the hard ground and nodded.

'From the look of those raiders, I thought you wouldn't last this long. But I guess they're just waiting for you to get the gold before they make their move.'

Crane suppressed a wince. 'Perhaps you're right. Did you figure out who they are?'

'It's a long story.'

'And I got time to hear it.'

'Put it this way — you're facing some tough opposition and explaining more than that won't help you none.' Lincoln raised a hand as Crane grunted his irritation. 'The important thing is I've found a safe route out of here.'

Truman looked up, rubbing his ribs.

'Listen to the man, Crane,' he said. 'He speaks sense. Leave now.'

'We ain't,' Crane grunted. 'As Lincoln said — I can think of fifty thousand reasons to stay here. We're holding out, no problem, no problem at all.'

'But you know I'm right,' Lincoln said. 'They're just waiting until you have the gold. Then they'll move on you.'

'Perhaps. But stop telling me bad news and tell me how we get away when we do have our gold.'

'For a start, if you keep your hostages, as soon as you get the gold, they'll be a burden. So, let them go. I've found a safe route back to Sweetwater they can take.'

Crane snorted. 'I ain't doing that.'

'When you confronted Truman in the trading post, you didn't want hostages, but now that you have them, they're just getting in the way and distracting you from defending this house properly.'

Crane glanced at Marvin, Seymour, then Truman, all of whom returned a hopeful smile.

'You're right. They are in the way, but

that doesn't mean they're leaving.'

'But, Crane, if one of them gets a stray bullet, all of you will swing whether you get the gold or not. Those raiders are only interested in you. And, if you let the hostages go, you'll find it easier to defend yourself.'

'And they'll just raise the alarm back in Sweetwater.'

'It's twelve miles to Sweetwater and it's sundown in less than an hour. By the time they've raised the alarm, it'll be dark and those raiders will have come. Before the law arrives, you'll either be long gone with the gold, or be dead.'

Truman paused from poking at the fire's dying embers.

'He speaks a lot of sense,' he said. 'You're more decent than this, Crane. Let us go.'

'I'm not releasing my only advantage.'

'Yeah,' Rocco muttered, 'we ain't siding with that.'

Crane winced as he stared at the

dying fire, then at his huddle of hostages.

'Once again, Rocco, your complaining has convinced me this is a good idea.' Crane pointed at the window. 'These people can go.'

Seymour and Marvin patted each other on the back.

'You made the right decision,' Lincoln said.

'But Truman stays until we reach our gold.'

'But you have to let them all — '

'That satisfies me,' Truman said. He rolled to his feet, clutching his ribs, then straightened, a momentary wince contorting his features. 'I brought this situation on myself when I reburied the gold.'

Lincoln sighed, then nodded. 'I guess you did.'

While wringing their hands, Marvin and Seymour glanced at Truman, but when Truman returned a comforting smile, they offered their encouragement and consolations.

Then, one at a time, they backed to the window and with Lincoln's help, climbed outside.

Crane sauntered up to Truman. 'Remember this — as soon as we have our gold, you can leave, too. So, dig.'

Truman winced, then grabbed the spade Marvin had dropped and lowered himself into the hole. He pushed the embers to one side and shovelled the earth, but the spade hit the ground with a solid thud.

'We need cover to escape,' Lincoln said by the window, then levered himself up on to the window ledge.

Crane nodded. 'And then?'

'And then I'll return and help you end this.' Lincoln nodded to Crane, then rolled from the window and dashed away.

13

Twenty yards from the summer house, Lincoln stopped by a large boulder and waited for Seymour and Marvin to reach him.

'The fog is all but cleared,' he said, 'and as soon we're another dozen or so yards from the house, Zandana's men will be able to see us. But like I said, I've found a safe route.'

Lincoln gathered Seymour and Marvin to his side and pointed to the side of the ridge, tracing a route with his finger that would afford them the maximum amount of cover.

'Seems possible,' Seymour said.

'It is. Now, we'll get covering fire. So, put your heads down and keep running. And don't look back or stop no matter what you hear.'

Marvin nodded, then Seymour. Lincoln directed them to stand on either side of him and, on the count of three, they scurried in a direct line for the ridge.

They had run for just ten paces when gunfire blasted from the other side of the summer house.

Lincoln didn't wait to see if the gunfire came from Crane or from Zandana, and instead, hurtled with his head down at right angles to the house, heading for the ridge.

At full pace they dashed until they reached the first onset of rocks. There, Lincoln checked that Zandana and his deputies hadn't moved, then picked out the route which headed up the slope through a winding path of large rocks, and which would hide him from most directions.

Lincoln headed up the slope in the lead. He maintained a brisk climbing pace, not wasting time encouraging the others to hurry.

Halfway to the top of the ridge, he edged to the side and peered over a large boulder, discovering that he was high enough to look down at Zandana's men below.

To his delight, they weren't looking at him, all their attention being on the house.

Lincoln backed from his position and doubled over, continued his journey up the slope.

Around a hundred yards from the top, beneath the sheer part of the ridge, he called a halt.

'Thanks for getting us out,' Seymour said, pacing up the last of the incline to stand beside him. 'But you're not leaving Truman in there, are you?'

'Nope.' Lincoln smiled. 'I have a plan to get him out safely and avoid those raiders killing anyone. But for my plan to work, you have to return to Sweetwater and organize help to come — and as quickly as possible.'

'But like Crane said, it's twelve miles to Sweetwater.'

'And by stagecoach it won't take long.' Lincoln pointed to the top of ridge. 'The stagecoach is about a half-mile on from the other side of the ridge.'

'And are my horses there?' Marvin asked.

'Yeah.'

Marvin punched the air, smiling broadly. 'In that case, I'll have help on the way back here faster than you can believe.'

With a last encouraging pat on the back to Marvin and Seymour, Lincoln left them to head around the side of the sheer part of the ridge while he scouted round below it.

He ran behind Zandana's position and headed for a large flat boulder where he could look down on the scene below.

But when he was twenty yards from the boulder, Zandana leapt up and sighted him down his rifle.

From nearly 300 yards away, Lincoln reckoned he'd be safe. But Zandana's first shot winged over Lincoln's head, close enough for him to imagine he felt a waft of air, and he thrust his head down to sprint the last few paces and leapt on to the flat boulder.

He lay a moment, then on his belly, snaked to the edge.

He ventured a glance and confirmed that below, Zandana had ducked beneath his cover again.

Lincoln shuffled into a more comfortable position with his head averted from the low sun, and reviewed the situation.

Around a hundred yards from the house, Zandana and his men had splayed out behind a sprawl of covering boulders. One deputy was to the side in a hollow that afforded him enough cover from the house, but not enough that he dared to move.

From that distance they were unlikely to hit anyone in the house if they were foolish enough to glance outside, but they could ensure that Crane didn't make a break from the front.

But as Lincoln had escaped from the back, the most likely explanation of Zandana's tactics was that he was encouraging Crane to run that way, and when weighted down with the recovered gold, he was backing himself to capture him.

A hand slapped on Lincoln's shoulder.

Although he was expecting it, Lincoln still flinched, then rolled on to his side.

Knelt behind him was Decker.

'Surprise you?' Decker asked, grinning.

'Nope, being as I asked you to cover me from here.'

Decker licked his lips. 'Just thought you might have expected me to run.'

'I didn't. I reckon you're a man who keeps his word, too.'

'Then you reckoned right.' Decker shuffled to the edge of the boulder and peered down the slope. 'But Zandana just wasn't interested in those hostages escaping or in you coming and going. He's only interested in Crane.'

'And the gold?'

'Yep.'

'I still ain't sure about all this.' Lincoln patted Decker's shoulder with a firm slap. 'But you did what you promised. You showed me a route that got the hostages to safety.'

'Twenty years ago, I hid out here for hours avoiding Zandana. The trees may have gone, but it's pretty much the same terrain.'

'And I'm obliged.' Lincoln turned from Decker and peered down the slope. 'And you can head off now.'

Decker sighted down the barrel of his gun at Zandana's position.

'Battle ain't over yet.'

Lincoln pointed down the ridge at the house.

'It ain't, but to win this, I won't need more firepower. I need to calm everyone down. So, just go. You'll have a few hours before a pursuit comes.' Lincoln shrugged. 'And it won't include me so you might stand a chance.'

'Obliged.' Decker hefted his gun, then shrugged and placed it on the boulder beside Lincoln, the gunbelt clattering down beside it a moment later. 'However calm you intend to be, I reckon you'll still need this.'

Lincoln smiled. 'Reckon as you're right.'

Decker tipped his hat, then crawled across the boulder. Ten yards from the edge he stood and scurried away, dashing from boulder to boulder.

Lincoln watched him wend a snaking path up the side of the ridge, following the path Marvin and Seymour had taken. He confirmed that none of Zandana's men was following him then, when he disappeared over the top, turned and peered down the slope.

Below, both groups were intractably trapped in their positions.

And that meant that the stand-off could remain at the same low level until Marvin and Seymour raised help back in Sweetwater.

He was still unsure as to whether Zandana was after the gold, or just after Crane. But Zandana's indifference at the hostages escaping, and therefore his seeming approval of the word about this siege spreading, had improved the chances that he was only after Crane.

So, Lincoln reckoned he had to give him the benefit of the doubt. And now felt the right time to prove whether his hunches were valid.

Lincoln took a deep breath, then stood and paced back from the edge of the boulder.

With his hands held high and his gun pointed to the sky, he paced on a determined route down the slope, but this time, he ensured that he stayed within Zandana's view.

Ahead, sporadic gunfire blasted from the house and from Zandana's position as the two opposing groups traded shots, but then Zandana saw Lincoln heading towards them and with a roar, ordered his deputies to still their fire.

His deputies stopped instantly. Two more shots ripped from the house before quiet descended.

'What in tarnation are you doing, Lincoln?' Zandana yelled, peering at

Lincoln from over a boulder and sighting him down the barrel of his rifle.

To avoid losing his footing on the slippery scree, Lincoln continued his steady pacing until he was at ground level, then edged sideways towards the house, ensuring he faced Zandana.

'I said,' Zandana roared, 'what are you doing?'

'I'm ending this stand-off with everyone still alive,' Lincoln shouted.

'And where's your fellow escapee?'

'He escaped. But I've returned.'

'And Raul?'

'Raul is secure and alive on the other side of the ridge.'

'Then that'll count in your favour. But you'll be the first to die if you don't give yourself up.'

'I ain't doing that. I'm just heading to the house to end this stand-off, and end it peacefully.'

Zandana snorted. 'I guess as you're a lawman you're planning to get the last of the hostages out?'

With Zandana mentioning his true role loud enough for Crane to hear, Lincoln winced and glanced at the house. He couldn't see who was covering the door, but when on the count of ten, no gunfire had emerged from within, he shrugged and held his head high.

'Yep. Although I've heard from some that you were planning to kill everyone once you have the gold, then keep it.' Lincoln smiled. 'But I didn't believe that.'

'You were right not to.'

'I guessed as much. But it doesn't matter now. Whatever the truth, this ends the same way with the gold returning to its owners, and all of Crane's hostages going free.'

'You got some of them out and I'm pleased to see that,' Zandana chuckled. 'Perhaps you are a lawman after all.'

'I am. And I directed those hostages to the stagecoach on the other side of the ridge and in about fifteen minutes, they'll be back in Sweetwater. And if you ain't honest lawmen, you won't be able to kill everyone here, then claim that what happened here was a raider attack, because there'll be witnesses back in Sweetwater whom you'll never silence.'

Zandana lowered his head behind his covering rock, presumably to talk to one of his deputies. Then he rose.

'You reckon you've figured everything out, don't you, Lincoln?'

'Yep.'

'And you reckon you've forced me to react in a way of your choosing?'

'Yep.'

'Then it's a pity for you that you're wrong.'

Zandana hurled his rifle to his shoulder and blasted a slug at Lincoln, but it winged over Lincoln's right shoulder.

As one, the deputies surged to their feet and ripped gunfire at him. Lead scythed through a trailing jacket sleeve, the rest ripping through the air around his head.

Lincoln winced. He glanced left and right. But as he was closer to the house than the nearest cover, he hurtled for the house.

Gunfire blasted at his heels, ripping dirt into the backs of his legs, but he thrust his head down and charged the last ten yards, his feet pounding to the ground and hurling up dust in his frantic dash.

Another volley ripped over his head, but he threw his hands up and dived into the house, skidding across the porch and through the doorway on his belly as another ripple of gunfire blasted across the doorway.

Lincoln skidded on the ground to plough into the side wall. He shook himself, confirming that he'd survived his mad dash, then sat up.

But it was only to face Rocco and the gun he'd aimed at his head.

14

'So,' Rocco muttered, 'you're a lawman, are you?'

Crane wandered from the doorway to stand beside Rocco as Lincoln jutted his jaw.

'Yeah,' Lincoln said. 'And if you were listening to all that, so are the men out there — they're Marshal Zandana and his deputies.'

'It is Zandana,' Rocco roared, glaring at Crane, who closed his eyes a moment. 'I've waited twenty years to get him.'

'But you can't take him on. You have to give yourself up.'

Crane sneered. 'We can't do that.'

Lincoln raised his gun hand so that he pressed the gun flat to the wall, pointing upwards.

'See sense and you'll get out of this alive.'

Crane strode before Rocco. 'You're in no position to threaten us.'

'And I ain't threatening you.' Lincoln pointed through the door with his left hand. 'But Zandana is sure threatening you.'

'And you reckon you can get us out of here alive?'

'Yep.'

'Then you're lying. Your negotiations with Zandana failed.' Crane smirked as Lincoln winced. He glanced over his shoulder. 'You hear that, Truman? Dig faster.'

'That won't help,' Lincoln said. 'You won't get the gold. You just ain't got the time to dig it up, get past Zandana, and escape the posse who're coming.'

Crane lowered his head, muttering to himself.

Rocco snorted. 'We still have Truman and you to negotiate with.'

'But you still won't escape with the gold. Too many people know about it now and you got no option but to walk away.'

Rocco grunted his indifference, but Crane raised his head.

'You're as misguided as Truman is,' Crane said. 'You can't expect us to give up on our gold after twenty years.'

Lincoln rolled to his feet, still keeping his gun aimed high.

'I can when it's the only option that will keep you alive and out of jail.'

'After what we've done here, if we live, we're returning to jail.'

'You don't have to. You did twenty years for failing to steal the gold buried in this house. I'm guessing you can't do more time for failing to steal it all over again.'

'I doubt that. We held people hostage and fired at lawmen.'

'Truman probably deserved it and Zandana and his deputies ain't decent enough for that to worry anyone. Just walk away. You've wasted enough of your life over that gold.'

Crane sighed. 'I wish I could believe that was the right thing to do.'

'Decker Calhoun did. He chose life over gold.'

Crane narrowed his eyes. 'When did you meet him?'

'Zandana brought him along to help him find the gold, except I escaped Zandana's clutches with him.' Lincoln shrugged his sleeves higher, displaying his broken handcuffs. 'Decker was all set to run, but when I promised I wouldn't pursue him, he helped me.'

'You wouldn't let Decker go.'

'I did, and he covered me when I first came in here.'

Crane glanced at Truman, who returned an encouraging nod, then at the hole, which despite everyone's efforts was still not softening or becoming deep enough to reveal the gold.

'I believe you're trying to end this stand-off without bloodshed,' he murmured. 'But walking away won't work.'

'It can if we trust each other.'

'Trust ain't the problem.' Crane shook his head and fixed Lincoln with his firm gaze. 'You got Seymour and Marvin out of here so that the lawmen couldn't silence them, didn't you?'

'Yep.'

'And you also told them to alert the law in Sweetwater so that they'll head here and end this siege?'

'That was my plan.'

Crane snorted, his sound echoed by Wallace and Elwood. Rocco threw back his head and roared with laughter.

'Then it was the stupidest plan I've ever heard,' Crane said, shaking his head. 'That help ain't coming.'

'Marvin will get to his stagecoach and raise the alarm in Sweetwater. Zandana didn't purse him.'

'Marvin might get to his stagecoach,' Crane said, his voice tired, 'and he might even head to Sweetwater and keep himself safe. But he won't fetch any reinforcements, and he will stop Seymour bringing any either.'

'Why?'

'Because Marvin works for me.'

'He doesn't,' Lincoln murmured.

'He's a decent man. I've ridden the stagecoach to Sweetwater with him before.'

'And that's what he does now, but that wasn't what he did twenty years ago.'

Lincoln gritted his teeth. 'You mean he was a member of the Calhoun gang?'

'Not exactly. Before Zandana captured Decker twenty years ago, Decker hired Marvin to transport the stolen gold. When we learnt that Marvin was driving the stagecoach to Sweetwater and that Truman Garner was on it, we told him to stop somewhere where we could confront him.' Crane shrugged. 'Why else do you think the stagecoach stopped at a trading post when Sweetwater is only fifteen miles away? And how else did you expect us to transport the gold when we'd found it?'

'I did wonder. But you're saying Marvin won't fetch help?'

'Nope.'

'Damn,' Lincoln murmured.

'So, knowing that, what do you reckon we do?'

Lincoln glanced around the small building, then sighed.

'At least Zandana doesn't know that Marvin will help you. So, he still thinks that help is a-coming. And that'll force him to act before sundown.'

'That doesn't help none.'

Gunfire roared outside, a stray bullet hurtling through the open doorway to rip into the facing wall.

In an involuntary action, Crane ducked and joined Lincoln in pressing himself flat against the side wall.

'But like I said,' Lincoln said. 'I've forced Zandana to act now.'

Crane sighed. 'Then I guess I have to ask — are you with us against Zandana?'

'Depends. Is Truman a free man?'

'If he lives through Zandana's onslaught, yeah.'

'And are you still after the gold?'

Crane glanced through the doorway into the adjoining room.

In the hole, Truman was chest high, but from the pained way that he was biting his bottom lip as he massaged his arms, he wasn't any closer to the gold.

'I guess not,' Crane whispered, then raised his voice and stood tall. 'I guess I never thought I'd say those words, but I don't need that gold.'

'Then I'm with you.'

Crane glanced at Rocco, whose mouth had fallen open, his face reddening by the second, but Crane turned from him and edged to the doorway.

Lincoln joined him in glancing outside. Framed before the rapidly sinking sun, Zandana and his deputies were dashing towards the house.

One of Zandana's deputies took up a position ten yards before the boulders behind which they'd been hiding. His fellow deputies maintained continuous fire at the house, forcing Lincoln to risk only the shortest of glances, and not enough to fire more than one wild shot.

Then each man dashed to an advanced position on the leading man and hunkered down, the other deputies covering the moving man.

At ten-yard intervals, they repeated the exercise, all the time closing on the house.

When the sprawl of deputies were twenty yards from the house, their frantic gunfire intensified around the doorway, forcing Crane to order everyone to stay back and not even venture returning fire.

By the door, Wallace twitched back and forth, but then in a momentary lull, he leapt into the doorway and blasted a single shot.

'Yeah, got one,' he cried, then spun around, a slug ripping into his chest and sending him plummeting to the ground.

Crane lurched out from his cover and grabbed his legs. With a sharp tug, he dragged him out of the way of further gunfire, but from the other side of the door, Lincoln could see that Wallace wasn't breathing.

Lincoln edged round the corner to fire, then leapt to the side, still firing, and rolled over his shoulder to take cover on the other side.

But all his gunfire was wild.

He repeated the wild action, dashing to the other side. Before he reached it his frantic finger twitching closed on an empty chamber, and Crane took his place, but intense gunfire from outside thundered through the open doorway and forced him to scurry for cover, too.

Then footsteps pounded outside and a deputy hurtled through the doorway, rolling over his shoulder as more of the deputies bundled in after him. Lincoln paused from his reloading to slug the nearest deputy to the jaw, then spun round to look for his next target.

Zandana was the last to leap through the door and Lincoln lurched for him, but another deputy bundled into him and knocked him to the ground.

Lincoln glanced around. In the confined space, the fighting was hand to hand. And with the numbers even, each deputy took on one of Crane's men.

Zandana had his back to Lincoln, trading blows with Crane. Lincoln leapt to his feet and immediately ducked under a wild blow from the deputy facing him, then grabbed Zandana in a bear-hug from behind. But Zandana thrust his elbow into Lincoln's guts, knocking him away.

Lincoln staggered back, but to his side, Rocco thundered a blow into his opponent that bundled the deputy into Lincoln.

Lincoln thrust out a leg and avoided falling. Then he swung back his fist and slugged the deputy to the ground. He reached down, ready to hurl the deputy through the doorway to the adjoining room, but from behind, Zandana grabbed his shoulder, swung him round, and smashed a blow into his jaw that crashed him into the wall.

As he rebounded, he saw Crane grab Truman's collar and hurl him through the front door, urging him to run. Then Crane swung round and hurled himself at Zandana. The two men went down in a heap.

To his side, Elwood was on the ground, his reddened hands clutching a knife sticking out of his chest.

But Rocco squared off to the man who had stabbed him and with one huge blow, slugged his jaw, sending him spinning back and through the doorway to the adjoining room. Then he swirled round to confront another deputy and with a long round-armed blow, hammered him through the doorway after the first man.

But this man tottered, then fell into the hole.

Lincoln turned to see Crane squirm out from beneath the prone Zandana and, with hope burgeoning in him that he might survive this battle, Lincoln leapt on Zandana's back and slammed his face into the ground, then again and again.

He glanced up to see that Crane had trained his gun down on them, waiting for an opening. But then the last of the deputies in the main room leapt to his feet and with both hands held together, crashed them down on Crane's back, knocking him to his knees.

As Crane floundered, the deputy ripped out his gun.

But Rocco turned on his heel and blasted a slug in the deputy's back as he fired, his last finger twitch gouging a bullet into the wall behind Crane's left shoulder before he fell against Crane. Then Rocco ducked as the deputies in the other room regrouped and fired at him through the doorway.

Lincoln dragged himself away from considering the other fights and concentrated on wrestling Zandana down.

But Zandana bucked him from his back, and as Lincoln floundered, he surged to his feet with a mighty roar and grabbed Lincoln's collar. Zandana dragged Lincoln to his feet and thundered a sickening blow into his guts, grinding his fist in a moment before ripping it back.

Lincoln folded over the blow and

staggered in a short circle, bile burning his throat. With no control of his movements, he walked into Zandana's right-arm slug to the jaw that sent him sprawling to the ground.

On the ground, Lincoln looked up to see Zandana tug his gun from its holster and aim it down at him.

But behind Zandana, Crane shrugged out from beneath the dead deputy, leapt to his feet, and kicked out, knocking Zandana's gun arm to the side and sending Zandana's blasted slug into the ground, inches from Lincoln's head.

Lincoln jerked to the side and rolled to his feet, then carried the movement on to bundle into Zandana and grab his gun arm. He pressed himself flat to Zandana's chest and thrust his arm high above their heads.

The two men flexed back and forth, but, inch by inch, Zandana dragged his gun down, past Lincoln's head, then in an arc, directing it inexorably in towards Lincoln's chest. But Crane jumped to Lincoln's side and grabbed the arm. And with Lincoln's help, he swung the arm back up.

Zandana grunted, his eyes bulging as he strained, but then he stamped his boot down on Crane's instep.

Crane winced, his grip momentarily weakening, and Zandana used the distraction to clip Crane's chin with his left hand.

Crane stumbled back, then tripped over a body, landing heavily on his side.

Lincoln and Zandana swung round to face each other, the gun jerking up and down as both men tried to gain control of it. A shot ripped into the roof. Then Zandana shuffled his feet to gain a firm stance and thrust the gun down between their two bodies.

Lincoln dragged the barrel from his chest and closed his hand around Zandana's hand, but then the two men slammed their chests together and a gunshot blasted, their bodies muffling the sound.

As hot fire momentarily burned Lincoln's chest, Zandana and Lincoln stared into each other's eyes.

Then Zandana's eyes rolled back and he slumped in Lincoln's grip. Lincoln opened his arms and, with slow inevitability, Zandana's gun fell from his slack fingers. He fell to his knees, then keeled over on to his back.

Crane fast-crawled to Zandana's side and grabbed the gun, then knelt by Zandana's body and felt his neck. He nodded to himself.

'That was for Decker,' he murmured.

Lincoln dashed to the corner. He reloaded, then joined Rocco in aiming his gun at the doorway to the adjoining room.

At his feet, Elwood was still, a bloom of blood darkening his chest.

Lincoln glanced around, counting the fallen, confirming that the only two standing deputies were in the adjoining room. And with three of them in this room, for the first time he believed that he'd survive.

'We got to end this,' Lincoln shouted, sighting the doorway down the barrel of his gun. 'Zandana is down.'

'You'll swing for that,' one of the deputies shouted, his voice sounding as if he'd pressed himself flat to the wall.

Crane staggered from the dead Zandana and joined Rocco and Lincoln in peering at the door, waiting for one of the deputies to show.

'Believe him. He's a lawman,' Crane shouted. He glanced at Elwood's body and sighed. 'And believe this — we've had enough of this fight and we can end this without further bloodshed.'

As Rocco snorted, Lincoln patted his back, smiling.

'Lincoln ain't no lawman,' the deputy shouted. 'And you'll pay for what you've done.'

'But he is,' a level voice said from the outside doorway. 'And he won't.'

15

Lincoln swirled round to face the doorway where Raul stood, the setting sun reddening his bulky outline and glinting off the chains dangling from his wrist.

'It's time we gave up,' Raul said, glancing at Zandana's body. 'Lawmen don't kill their own kind.'

'He ain't no lawman,' one of the deputies shouted.

Raul paced into the house and stood over Zandana's body.

'He is. He didn't kill me when he could have, and if he was the man Zandana reckoned he was, he wouldn't have done that.'

'But we can't end this. You know that.'

'You can,' Lincoln said, rolling to his feet. 'Raul's right. You men have a choice. You ain't getting the gold without word of this fight getting out. You got no choice but to end this now and convince me that you were always intending to turn the gold in.'

Muttering sounded from the adjoining room.

'We did intend to turn the gold in.'

Lincoln smiled at the deputy's less-than-convincing tone, but he firmed his own voice.

'Then come out and I'll believe you.'

'Throw down your guns and we will.'

'No deals. I'm the lawman in charge here now and you do what I say.'

More muttering sounded, but with another muttered plea from Raul, in single file the two deputies paced out, their guns held high. With a last glance at Raul, who provided an encouraging nod, they opened their hands and let their guns fall at their feet.

'And now you two,' Lincoln said, looking at Crane, then Rocco. 'You've already made the right decision. Just end this.'

'And we can go?' Crane asked,

turning to Lincoln.

'I guess I did promise that.' Lincoln glanced around the room at the bodies. 'I'll have to distort the truth a mighty lot if I'm to deliver on all my promises, and I guess that'll be easier if you've gone.'

'No problem,' Crane murmured. He glanced at his gun, then shrugged and raised his gun hand. He glanced at Rocco. 'Come on, Rocco. This is over.'

'I ain't accepting that,' Rocco muttered, his eyes blazing. 'We must be getting near our gold.'

Crane snorted. 'I reckon we could dig forever and we wouldn't reach that gold. Admit defeat.'

Rocco hunched his shoulders, his harsh breath snorting through his nostrils as he hefted his gun in his right hand. Then he swirled round and turned his gun on Lincoln.

'I ain't,' he roared, his eyes wide and blazing. 'I'm getting my gold.'

'Don't do this,' Lincoln said. 'You ain't getting the gold, and acting real stupid now will just get you killed.'

'Brave talk when you're facing my gun,' Rocco yelled. He spat on the ground, then stalked backwards to the door, stopping when he'd ensured that he had everyone in the room in his view. 'But I came for my gold. And you'll dig it up for me.'

'Rocco, don't,' Crane murmured.

'I ain't listening.'

Crane sighed. 'Truman always said it'd come to this. And I guess he was right.'

'What's that supposed to mean?'

'It means Lincoln has given us a way out with none of us returning to jail, and I reckon I'll take it. And if you don't — '

'And I ain't.' Rocco turned his gaze on Crane and sneered. 'But I guess you were right. It was always coming to this. So, if you want to take me on, do it, but I'm leaving with my gold, or dying in the attempt.'

Lincoln and Crane glanced at each other. They'd both aimed their guns at the roof, but Lincoln directed a short shake of his head towards Crane.

'Then it'll be dying,' Lincoln said. 'Because you can't take on both of us before one of us stops you.'

'That won't matter to the one I kill.'

'Rocco,' Crane said, 'nobody has to die.'

Rocco snorted, then swirled his gun from Lincoln to aim it at Crane.

Lincoln thrust his gun down but before he could turn it on Rocco, a gunshot ripped out, the noise echoing in the small room.

Lincoln trained his gun on Rocco, but didn't fire as Rocco staggered forward a pace, then stumbled to his knees and keeled over on to his front, clutching his chest.

He glanced at Crane, but he still had his gun aimed high. Lincoln swung round, searching for the shooter, but the deputies had their hands high, too.

But then he saw him.

Standing behind Rocco in the doorway was Decker Calhoun. A flurry of smoke rose from his gun barrel.

'You returned,' Lincoln said.

'Yep,' Decker said.

'And where did you get that gun?'

'There was a body outside.' Decker flashed a smile.

'Then I'm obliged.' Lincoln glanced at Decker's gun. 'But you ain't returned to do anything stupid have you?'

'Nope. I always said you should never kill.' Decker tipped back his hat and rubbed his eyes. 'But in Rocco's case . . . '

Crane turned and appraised Decker.

'And I'm mighty pleased you found the exception,' he said, a huge grin emerging.

As Crane and Decker patted each other's backs, Lincoln wended past them to stand in the doorway.

'Then if we're all in agreement that you're forgetting about the gold,' Lincoln said. 'I have to head to Sweetwater and fetch the law.'

'No need,' Decker said. 'The law will be here within minutes. I caught up with Marvin and *persuaded* him to do the right thing. Seymour headed to Sweetwater on one of his horses.'

'Then I'm even more obliged.'

'Boss,' Crane said, standing back from Decker, 'what are your orders?'

'We wasted twenty years dreaming about the gold that got away,' Decker said. 'Now we start living.'

'And what about us?' Raul murmured.

'The way I see it,' Lincoln said, 'you ambushed Elwood and Wallace, thinking they had the stolen gold. But once Zandana got himself killed, you and I resolved the stand-off.'

'And who killed Zandana?'

'I did.' Lincoln folded his arms as he faced Raul. 'But then again, I didn't reckon he was a lawman when I killed him.'

16

'So,' Crane said, mounting one of Zandana's spare horses, 'you're saying we leave the gold where it is?'

Decker nodded. He mounted another spare horse and turned it to stand beside Crane.

'Yep. Freedom is a whole lot better than wasting your life on a past mistake.'

'I ain't sure you're right there.' Crane glanced at the deputies who were wandering from the summer house, and imagined just how many lawmen would arrive here shortly. 'But I guess we ain't got much choice — that gold is plain buried too deep.'

'Either way, you made the right decision.'

'Then I'm with you. Where are we going?'

'North.'

'Sounds good to ... ' Crane narrowed his eyes as he saw a figure emerge from behind a boulder, 200 yards up the ridge. He snorted as he confirmed that the figure was Truman.

Truman peered at him, his hands raised ready to dive for cover, but Crane beckoned him on, as did Lincoln from the house.

'Come on,' Decker said. 'Forget him.'

'I will, but I just have to ask him something before we leave.'

Crane dismounted. He passed his reins to Decker, then stood with his arms folded, ten yards before the house, watching Truman scamper down the ridge, then pace towards him when he reached flat ground.

'So,' Truman said, coming to a halt before him, 'you decided to take my advice.'

'I guess I did.' Crane glanced to the north. 'I chose life, not gold.'

'Then you made the right choice — as I knew you would.'

'I hope so.' Crane set his hands on

his hips. 'But before I go, you have to tell me one thing.'

Truman laughed. 'I know what you want to ask and my answer still stands. The gold is in my summer house.'

Crane shook his head and turned. He wandered back to the house, Truman following him. With his head down, he paced into the house to stand two feet in from the doorway.

For the last time, he peered through the doorway at the hole, trying but failing to imagine the gold just inches below the bottom of the hole.

'And how much further would we have had to dig down before we reached it?'

Truman joined him in peering at the hole. 'Would knowing make you sleep any easier?'

Crane sighed. 'Probably not. But tell me anyhow.'

Truman turned and leaned back on the doorway.

'I've heard it said that there are gold seams in these hills. Maybe if you'd dug down far enough you might have reached one.'

Crane winced. 'You saying we were digging in the wrong place?'

'Yes.'

'But the gold is still in the summer house?'

Truman ran his gaze along the wall, picking out the numerous bullet holes that peppered the walls.

'It is.'

Crane followed Truman's gaze, but then shrugged.

'I wish I could believe you, but after all the disappointment . . . '

'Believe me.'

Crane tipped back his hat, sighing, then turned and headed outside. He nodded to Lincoln, then mounted his horse and with Decker leading, headed north, the start of one of the golden sundowns Truman had promised glowing to his left.

'So,' Decker said, glancing at Crane with a lively gaze, 'how close were you to the gold?'

'As far as I ever was.'

'But it was there?'

'Yeah, the gold was in the summer house.'

Crane glanced over his shoulder. The last rays of sunshine were rippling in deep red arcs across the summerhouse walls and just for a moment the whole building glowed gold. 'And it seems like Truman will be enjoying another golden sundown.'

'And you should stop looking so glum,' Decker said.

'You can't stop me dreaming of what might have been.'

'Perhaps not.' Decker leaned towards Crane. 'But that's the difference between you and me. You've spent the last twenty years dreaming about what you could do with the gold when you left jail and dug it up again.'

'Whereas you just dreamt of being free?'

'Nope.' Decker leaned to the side and winked. 'I spent my time working out where I went wrong with the raid in the first place.'

Crane snorted. 'And you've figured that out, have you?'

'Yep.' Decker lowered his voice. 'And I won't make the same mistake next time.'

Crane narrowed his eyes. 'Next time?'

'Ain't no use worrying about reclaiming that gold.' Decker pointed forward then hurried his horse to a trot. 'We just have to raid another gold shipment, and this time, we'll succeed. You with me?'

Crane hurried on to join Decker, a smile tugging at his mouth.

'I sure am,' he hollered. 'We'll show those young 'uns how to do it.'

★   ★   ★

Lincoln watched Decker and Crane ride away.

He had gone against his natural instincts and let known outlaws escape justice, but in this case, he was sure it was the right decision.

'The law from Sweetwater,' Truman

221

murmured, pacing to Lincoln's side.

Lincoln put a hand to his brow and looked to the sundown, and as the sun disappeared below the low clouds on the horizon, from around the ridge, he saw the trail of riders galloping towards them.

Lincoln turned to Truman. 'You got your story right in your mind, too?'

Truman wandered back to his house and patted the side of the doorway.

'Yeah. I'll own up about what I did and hand over the gold. Then I guess I'll rebuild my summer house.'

Lincoln glanced at the bullet holes around the door.

'It ain't that badly damaged.'

'Yet.'

Truman glanced in the direction of Lincoln's gaze, then poked in a bullet hole. He shook his head and sauntered inside, muttering about the damage to his summer house.

Lincoln nodded and stood a moment, staring at the house.

Then, from behind the clouds hugging the horizon, the dying sun poked through, bathing the summer house in the day's last rays and for just a moment something glittered, then was gone when the sun slid below the horizon.

Lincoln shook his head, almost dismissing the sight as a fanciful vision.

Then he saw it.

The bullet holes had dug deep into the adobe walls, and deep within one of the holes, a hint of gold gleamed.

Lincoln nodded to himself and turned to face the approaching riders.

'Like Truman said,' Lincoln whispered to himself, 'the gold *was* in the summer house.'

We do hope that you have enjoyed reading this large print book.

Did you know that all of our titles are available for purchase?

We publish a wide range of high quality large print books including:
Romances, Mysteries, Classics
General Fiction
Non Fiction and Westerns

Special interest titles available in large print are:
The Little Oxford Dictionary
Music Book, Song Book
Hymn Book, Service Book

Also available from us courtesy of Oxford University Press:
Young Readers' Dictionary
(large print edition)
Young Readers' Thesaurus
(large print edition)

For further information or a free brochure, please contact us at:
Ulverscroft Large Print Books Ltd.,
The Green, Bradgate Road, Anstey,
Leicester, LE7 7FU, England.
Tel: (00 44) **0116 236 4325**
Fax: (00 44) **0116 234 0205**

BLADE LAW

Jack Reason

A silver necklet was all that was left to identify the body of the man McKee found dead in the mountains. The brutal murder was the work of Juan Darringo and his bandits who had made the mountain ranges their lair of robbery and death . . . However, identification of the dead man was to lead McKee back to the mountains accompanied by a man intent on retribution. Now, forced to pit their wits against the cruel terrain, they also find themselves the prey in a hunt that will have only one outcome.